PENNY OATES

---◆---

TO TRUST
AND BE TRUE

Complete and Unabridged

LINFORD
Leicester

First published in Great Britain in 2019

First Linford Edition
published 2020

A catalogue record for this book is available
from the British Library.

ISBN 978–1–4448–4430–6

Published by
Ulverscroft Limited
Anstey, Leicestershire

Set by Words & Graphics Ltd.
Anstey, Leicestershire
Printed and bound in Great Britain by
T. J. International Ltd., Padstow, Cornwall

This book is printed on acid-free paper

TO TRUST AND BE TRUE

Jennie Wright hopes for a new start as a live-in carer for the semi-comatose Race Engleton at a remote country estate — where she is soon surrounded in mystery. Race's niece Kira and her handsome brother Wren are also in residence and seem to be concealing a secret, while the family doctor's prescribed medication is doing Race more harm than good. In the meantime, Jennie is caught between her attraction to Wren and the attentions of Doug, a local tree surgeon. But who, if anyone, can she trust?

1

When I think back to the extraordinary events that took place at Great Haddows, it seems only right that the first time I ever saw the house it had been shrouded in mists and shadows.

I remember I shivered as I watched the retreating headlights of the taxi that had delivered me. I felt very alone, sandwiched as I was between the twin clipped yew bushes that stood sentinel on either side of the front door. It was late and I had been lucky to find a driver willing to make the country journey along the winding road at that time of night. I knew I was, because he had told me so constantly the entire journey. Yet even though his incessant whining had grated — he was getting well paid for his efforts, after all — when we arrived and viewed that grand mansion, I felt vulnerable and didn't

1

really want to get out.

It appeared dark and forbidding with only a weak porch light that barely illuminated the door bell, and as the taxi wended its way back down the long drive, the driver eager to be home, I was hard pressed not to go running after him. Which was strange, because I am not normally given to flights of fancy, but I can't help but wonder if the disquiet I felt at first acquaintance with the old building was not due to the evil that, unbeknown to me then, was being played out inside.

Whatever my misgivings, I knew I couldn't run away. I needed this job. I no longer had a home to call my own, had no career, and during the bitter-sweet years of caring for my parents my friends had dropped away, as friends will when you are never able to go out with them.

I was hoping that a year at Great Haddows would help get me back on track so I could decide what I wanted to do with my life and plan how I should go about achieving it.

I took a deep breath, pushed the ancient button in and waited for the door to be opened.

Utter silence.

I hadn't heard the bell ring, but that wasn't surprising given the size of the house. I expected it had sounded in some distant servants' quarters. But when no one had answered after a few minutes, I was left in that uncomfortable position of not knowing if anyone had heard and debating whether it would appear impatient or rude to ring again if they had.

I was just about to do so, when the door was flung wide and welcome pools of warm golden light chased the shadows away. But warmer still was the smile that greeted me, and I felt the air escape from my lungs as I beheld the handsomest man I had ever met. Rarely does one come face to face with perfection but it seemed to me then that I had just done so.

With his dark hair, green eyes and

mischievously mocking expression — as though he was aware of the effect his good looks had on all who saw him and was amused by it — I found myself completely tongue-tied.

'Oh, hello . . . em . . . I'm . . . I'm Jennie Wright,' I stammered, inwardly berating myself for my gauche behaviour. I was twenty-three years old, for goodness sake, and hardly an ingénue.

He grinned. 'Thought you must be — we don't get many casual callers at midnight in this neck of the woods! I'm Wren Engleton.'

So this was my new employer's nephew; the agency had told me about him and his sister. He shook my hand with a firm but not bone-crushing grasp, before grabbing my suitcase.

'Come in, come in — it's freezing out there!'

It was. March had been a particularly cold month and so far, it seemed as if spring would never arrive. I stepped thankfully into the panelled hall, nervous and yet strangely excited, my

4

previous fears dismissed in an instant by an attractive face. I had read that people often equate physical beauty with all the best human gifts and emotions but I hadn't thought I could be so shallow; yet all my misgivings had dissolved in the light of his smile!

'This way.'

He led me to a large formal drawing-room where two women were sitting near the dying embers of a fire.

'This is my sister, Kira, and my uncle's housekeeper, Mary Kent.'

We all exchanged nods, and I was ushered to a chair beside the flickering logs.

'She's cold as a block of ice!' Wren exclaimed. 'Mary, could you get her a hot drink?'

'Of course.' Mary rose to her feet and gave me a polite smile. 'Would you like some Ovaltine?'

'That would be wonderful.'

And I meant it. People didn't often do things for me, I was usually the gofer myself. I didn't resent it — five years caring first for my father and then my mother as both succumbed to fatal illnesses had been a privilege but hard work nevertheless, so it was always a treat when I was waited on.

'We were expecting you earlier.' Kira eyed me up. It wasn't an unfriendly inspection, but she did seem more cautious than her brother.

'Oh, yes.' I realised I hadn't explained my late arrival. 'There was a points failure on the line which meant our train had to wait in sidings for two hours. I tried to phone, but there was no mobile signal all the way here, and when I wanted to use the call box at the station, the taxi driver threatened to leave if I didn't get in his car at once as it was so late and he was about to go off duty.'

I was gabbling, I knew, but this was the first real job I'd had, and I was nervous. Could I be blamed for the delayed train? I didn't really see how, but who knew?

'Hmm!' Wren snorted. 'I bet that was

John Hancock — I've discovered to my cost that he won't put himself out for anyone unless he's well paid. Was he driving an old London taxi?' I nodded. 'Complained all the way here, I expect. How much did he charge you?' I told him and he shook his head. 'Should have been half that. Never mind, you'll be driving the estate car in future so you won't have to call upon his services.'

I sent up a silent prayer of thanks to my father, who had insisted on teaching me how to drive even as his condition deteriorated.

'Your mother never did learn and someone's got to be able to get to the supermarket,' he'd joked. Briefly, I looked back on the private times we spent together in the car as he instructed me on the rules of the road as some of the closest we ever shared.

'Look after her, darling girl,' he'd said once, and of course I'd promised I would, although neither of us had known then how prescient his request was to be. Mum had required a great deal of looking after very soon after his death and I had definitely needed to drive her then — to the doctor's, later to the hospital, and finally to the hospice. When it was all over and I began to look for work, I discovered many clients required carers who could do similar journeys for them.

Wren rose and made for the door. 'Well, I'm off to bed now as I have to be in London early tomorrow. I'll take your case up and leave it in your room. Mary can show you where it is when she brings back your drink, and tomorrow she'll introduce you to Race.'

'Race?' I was puzzled.

'It's my uncle's nickname — short for Reginald Andrew Charles Engleton. He always hated his given name, my father told me, and when he was ten announced that in future he would only answer to Race. He was such a charmer that his family accepted it, and apparently he grew into the name — he was quite racy in his teens and twenties, though you wouldn't know it now, poor man.' He paused and gave a resigned shake of his head before continuing, 'Still, Mary makes sure he's as comfortable as possible, and that's why you're here, too.' He gave me a brief smile and I found myself bathing in its glow. 'I'm sure you won't find him much trouble, he just needs to be watched and Mary can show you the ropes.'

Somehow the room really did seem less bright once he left, which was ridiculous and worryingly unlike my normal down-to-earth character. I'm not the type of person to indulge in unrealistic daydreaming.

I saw that Kira had watched me watching Wren. She was a female version of her brother with classic bone structure and the same arresting eyes, but they were not as welcoming as his.

I wondered how the household was run and where I would fit in with the family and current staff. The agency that sent me had given minimal details: a gentleman living in his country house with young relatives requiring assistance at home. I had been told there was a housekeeper, so I would only be expected to provide care.

'As you did for your parents, dear,' Mrs Miller, the agency proprietor, had said. 'I know you don't have experience of doing so professionally, but the hospice gave you ever such a good reference based on the way you helped out there, so I'm sure everything will be fine.'

I hoped so too, but didn't share her confidence. I wasn't certain that I was cut out to be a paid carer and had the distinct impression Kira wasn't sure about me, either.

I suspected looking after 'a client' was going to be very different from looking after my own parents, but at that moment I didn't have a choice, so when Mary returned with my drink I gave Kira my best smile and bid her good night before following the housekeeper upstairs.

The house was clearly very old, with sloping oak floors and a rather higgledy-piddledy arrangement of corridors and steps; nowhere seemed to be all on one level.

'Built in the sixteenth century,' Mary advised when I asked her, 'and been in the Engleton family ever since. It has a lot of original features because they lost all their money soon after it was finished and so couldn't remodel it like most grand families did over the years. In fact, it was only after Mr Race and his wife took charge that things improved. They were very successful in business.' She opened a door and led me into an elegant bedroom. 'This will be your room. It's opposite Mr Race's suite, so if necessary you can get to him easily in the night.'

'What time should I get up?'

'Mr Race wakes at about eight-thirty. If you want to come down to the kitchen before that I'll make you some breakfast and then introduce you. Kira won't be up before ten as she doesn't start work until lunchtime tomorrow.'

Her expression left no doubt as to what she thought of such tardiness.

'Good night then, Mary, and thank you.'

I was glad when she left. It had been a long day and I was very tired.

I looked around the room she had brought me to. It was twice as large as my parents' double bedroom had been at home, with a dressing-room and en suite bathroom attached.

I was somewhat dismayed to discover the dressing-room also had an exit to the outside landing, so that even if I locked the bedroom door there would be another way in. I gave myself a mental shake — why was I concerned? Who did I think might try the door — Wren Engleton? That was surely a bad case of wishful thinking!

Happily ignorant of the real situation, I was sure there was nothing to worry about. I decided I would unpack properly the next day, actually remembered to plug in my mobile phone to charge, and fell thankfully into bed.

★ ★ ★

The next morning I woke early, momentarily confused about where I was.

Then I remembered, and a nervousness overtook me as I considered what it might be like to live and work in someone else's house. What would be expected of me? Would I be required to be on call twenty-four hours a day, and for how many days? Would I even have days off?

Mrs Miller had been vague at my interview and I had not asked, being too numb from my losses, not only of Dad and Mum, but also of the happy home we had shared. Dad's illness had prevented him from working for many months and his savings had tided us along until Mum died, but when she passed I'd had to face the fact that the mortgage was in arrears and the cottage would have to be sold.

When everything had been paid off there wasn't even enough left over for the necessary down payment to secure a rented studio, so I had been rather desperate when I approached the care agency. It had been the bereavement counsellor at the hospice who had suggested I did so when I told her that I soon would have nowhere to live.

'You showed a natural talent for caring,' she had said, 'and you could find a live-in position just to give you breathing space until you decide what you want to do. I could introduce you to an agency I know and give you a reference.'

As there was nothing else I had agreed, but now that I was here at Great Haddows, I wondered if I had made a dreadful mistake.

I knew nothing about these people, had no idea of my terms and conditions of employment and felt very cut off from the rest of the world. The house stood alone in a Kentish valley with no near neighbours, and remembering the winding pass the taxi had travelled the previous evening, I wondered how easy it would be to get out and about. I hadn't noticed any bus stops on my journey here.

I wandered over to the latticed window and peered out . . . and at once my spirits lifted. It was a bright but icy early spring morning with a ground frost silvering the gardens. They were formal and well-tended with plants pruned, staked and mulched in much the same way my mother had cared for our cottage garden, although on a much smaller scale. She had loved gardening and it was a passion she passed on to me. I had been all set to do a degree in horticulture when Dad became ill. There had been no question but that I would defer until things at home were more stable, yet fate had intervened and that time had never come.

I stared out over the grounds, noting a small cottage to the right next to a tennis court, and a walled kitchen garden beyond.

To me there has always been something timeless and unending about gardens; the round of seasons with their particular tasks marking the passage of time, yet repeating annually so that they held a comforting familiarity. I never failed to find something soothing about working on the land. Without a home or even an allotment to call my own I had thought it was just another love I had lost, but perhaps it wasn't. Maybe I could help with the garden here and in a year or so reapply to university.

I took a quick shower and dressed ready to go downstairs.

Mary was frying eggs on the Aga and when I refused her offer of a cooked breakfast, pointed me in the direction of the cereals.

'Mr Race likes a cooked breakfast,' she said. 'We can take it up once you've finished.'

Together we went upstairs. I carried the tray and Mary rapped on the bedroom door before marching in.

'Hello, Mr Race,' she said with the forced cheerfulness of the professional carer that I had come to recognise — and dislike — from certain nurses at the hospice. 'I've got someone here to meet you.'

She indicated that I should set the tray down on a bed table, and then helped Race Engleton out of bed. He must once have been a fine figure of a man — he remained a tall one in spite of his hunched shoulders and rounded back — but now he relied on Mary to support him to the chair.

His grey hair was still thick and curly, and his angular face had the same fine bone structure as Wren and Kira — the good looks obviously came from the Engleton side of the family. But his eyes were markedly different; whereas theirs were sparking and vibrant, their uncle's were lifeless and disinterested.

Mrs Miller had told me Mr Engleton had developed an undefined neurological illness at the early age of fifty-eight and that he needed only general physical assistance rather than hands-on care. I had helped similar patients at the day centre Dad had attended, and had expected my client to resemble them. But he did not. I realised my task would be more that of a guardian than anything else.

Once he was settled in the armchair by his bed, Mary gave him some tablets, which he took without demur. Then she pulled the bed table in front of him.

'Pull up a chair,' she instructed me, 'and then you can encourage him to eat. You have to keep reminding him or he will simply forget to do so. Mr Race is unable to initiate things, so your role will be to prompt him constantly to ensure he stays safe and healthy.'

I forbore to say that he did not appear very healthy to me at the present time.

On the mantelpiece was a framed photograph of an extremely good-looking, vivacious man, clearly my client when younger. It seemed so unfair that someone who once must have been as lively and attractive as his nephew was reduced to this.

'I'll leave you to it,' Mary said. 'When he's finished, start running him a shower and tell him to undress and wash himself. He'll do so if you tell him to, but won't be able to start the process without your help. He's got a shower stool, so he'll be quite safe. You see that file by the bed? It contains information about Mr Race and guidance on how to manage him. Just follow what's written there and you'll be OK.'

I nodded, and once she'd gone, gently urged the stooped man to eat.

He did not appear to see me, never meeting my eyes, but he did as he was bid. I chatted to him, telling him about myself and occasionally asking him questions, which remained unanswered. I wondered if I was getting through to him, but even if he gave no indication that he knew I was there, I was determined to continue speaking to him as if he did.

I read the guidance file while he was showering. It gave clear instructions on the best way to approach Mr Engleton and how to get him to co-operate about the house, but I was surprised that the timetable set down made no allowance for any kind of life outside of his home and very little even outside his own suite of rooms. No wonder his eyes were so dead and his mind so empty if he never had the opportunity to do anything but a reduced routine of getting up, watching TV and going to bed!

I determined there and then that I would try and give him a more stimulating day.

'There now,' I said, as I settled him down in his armchair once he was dressed, 'I'll turn the TV on, but perhaps we can go for a walk in the garden when it's warmed up a bit.'

I expected no response and was not disappointed. The TV clicked on at my touch — straight to a cartoon. I frowned. Surely this wasn't his usual fodder, not for a grown man? But perhaps he responded to the humour?

I waited and watched for a while, but although his tired eyes were fixed on the wide screen he made no movement to suggest he was registering what was on. He shuffled in his seat to change his position and the controls fell from the arm of the chair where I had placed them down the side of the seat.

I realised this must be what had happened the last time the TV was on, and that the pressure from Mr Engleton's body must have accidentally changed the channel. No one would deliberately have tuned into a children's programme for him to watch.

I retrieved the controls and flicked over to the news. He gave no sign of noticing, but I left it on while I took the breakfast tray downstairs.

Kira was in the kitchen eating a slice of toast. In daylight her beauty was even more breath-taking, though she herself seemed oblivious to it.

'How was Race?' she asked as I stacked plates in the dishwasher.

I thought for a moment before replying. How would I describe him?

'Distressingly frail and distant,' I said at last.

She regarded me with her penetrating green eyes.

'Yes, that's just how he appears,' she

agreed. 'When I first met him I was as shocked as you obviously are, but we've been here six months now and Wren and I have become used to his condition.'

I was surprised. From what she was saying, Kira and her brother were newcomers at Great Haddows themselves.

'In his room there's a photo of your uncle as a handsome young man,' I said. 'When did he first become unwell?'

'I'm not sure. My father, Paul, was Race's younger brother, and they had some kind of falling-out in their twenties — I think about Race's wife, Susan. Dad emigrated to South Africa and had no contact until Race wrote to him after Aunt Susan died, nearly a year ago now. It took a while for the letter to find us as Race didn't have our current address so it only arrived last summer.'

She paused, as if remembering a time when life had been kinder.

'Dad wasn't that keen to visit, but blood is thicker than water, so he phoned Race and agreed to come over with Mum.'

'How was Mr Race then?'

'Fine, as far as I know. Leastways, Dad said he'd sounded anxious on the phone and was quite insistent they should meet up, but there was nothing to indicate Race was ill.'

'How did the meeting go?'

Kira sighed. 'By the time they got here Race was really unwell and hardly knew them. It made no difference to him.'

Her gaze faltered for a moment, and then she lifted her chin as if fixing her courage and went on, 'But it did to my parents. While they were here they decided to go to London one day, and Dad was driving Race's old sports car. At the inquest they said it was because he wasn't used to it, that he must have misjudged his speed. They skidded off the road and were both killed.'

She said it in a flat tone, as if unable to trust herself not to break down if she showed any emotion.

'I'm so sorry.' I knew how inadequate the words were, having heard them so often myself. 'It's unbearable at first, isn't it?'

She looked at me questioningly and then nodded. 'Of course, you've been in a similar situation, haven't you? It was ghastly, but somehow life goes on and you have to adjust.'

'Yes, I've found that.'

'Life is so arbitrary, don't you find?' she continued. 'There was my father, in the full flush of life — six years younger than Race — and he dies . . . whereas his brother, who barely has any quality of life at all, remains trapped in that shell of a body.'

She pulled a face, her expression a strange mixture of anger and resignation.

'If I were Race I'd want someone to put me out of my misery.'

I wasn't shocked exactly, but she said it with such vehemence that I wondered if she resented her uncle — blamed him for putting her parents in the situation where a freak accident had taken them from her.

I tried to sound non-committal. 'We can't really know how much he understands of his life.'

'Life!' she spat it out. 'You can't call *that* a life! Stuck up in his bedroom all day apart from a twice daily walk up and down the corridor!'

'Does he never do anything else?'

'Once a week a personal trainer comes and takes him through a range of exercises but that's about it. His doctor isn't keen for him to be outdoors in case he falls, and anyway, he says Race really couldn't cope with meeting other people and going out socially.'

'I suppose he knows what's best for him,' I said, though in truth, I was surprised. The doctors at the hospice had been keen that my parents should live as full a life as possible for as long as they could, and I wondered if the GP wasn't being over-protective.

Kira rose from the table and left the room, and I went to the back door to see what was outside.

It opened onto a paved patio beside a large natural pond with a duck house on its central island, where various wildfowl were happily ensconced.

A path led away from it, weaving between the trees towards the fields beyond. The frost had thawed and the ground looked reassuringly firm and I saw no reason why at some time in the future I shouldn't take Race — I found I was using his nickname myself — for a short walk. I could take a photo of the path and show the doctor how safe it would be, and I felt in my pocket for my mobile, only to find it empty. That was typical of me — not having had many people to call over the last few years I hadn't used my phone much so I tended to leave it all over our cottage rather than keeping it with me. It hadn't mattered then as invariably no one would have been trying to ring me. But now I was at Great Haddows I realised I needed to be contactable and resolved to be more assiduous in keeping it on me.

Still, there was no great rush to approach the doctor. I would need to bide my time and develop Race's trust before I could take him outside. I would not have considered doing so, had I thought I would be undermining some important treatment plan if I did. I had been brought up to respect authority, but Race was not immobile and the therapists at the day centre had impressed upon me that, where muscles were concerned, it was 'use it or lose it'. When I had feared my father might hurt himself his physiotherapist had put my mind at rest.

'Life is full of dangers,' she had said, 'Every time we cross a road we could be knocked down, but actually very few people are. So we assess the hazards your father encounters and adjust what we do to minimise them. For example, waiting until there are no cars coming before we cross the road! It's important we don't allow our own fears to prevent him from doing what is both dear to him and good for him.'

I had found her advice hard to accept at first. I might not have been given to fantastic notions, but I had always been a scaredy-cat, expecting — and preparing for — the worst.

As a much-wanted late arrival — I was born when my mother was in her forties — my parents had been determined to shield me from harm and impressed upon me the dangers that lurked around every corner. I knew they meant well, but it had left me extra-cautious and wary of doing anything that looked even slightly dangerous. So it had taken me some time to follow the therapist's lead. When I did, the improvement in my father's well-being was so pronounced that I was quickly won over.

In view of that, I was sure a little exercise could do Race no harm and would most probably be very good for him.

'I'll show you where we keep Mr Race's drugs.'

I hadn't heard Mary enter the

kitchen and I jumped. She walked over to a wall cupboard and took out a weekly dosette box.

'I keep the bottles under lock and key in my kitchen at the cottage and fill the dosette boxes once a week. That way there's no chance of a mistake being made. Just make sure you take the correct tablets for the right date and time.'

'What about signing to say I've given them?'

She turned to face me, a peeved expression on her face.

'There's no need for all that. Mr Race is in his own home. You're not a trained nurse and I've been overseeing his care for a good nine months now, so I don't need to be told how to do my job!'

I nodded, suitably chastened.

It appeared Mary resented the fact that I had been employed. I had assumed she would be pleased to have some relief, but perhaps she felt I would interfere with her routine. After all, having more experience than me, I could see it would be galling if a younger carer came in and tried to change everything. I determined to give her no cause to question my work.

★ ★ ★

Over the next few days Mary showed me the care regime to be followed and told me what was expected of me.

'Once you've got the hang of things you'll sometimes be left in sole charge of Mr Race,' she explained. 'I'll also want you to drive to town to do the shopping on occasion. Dawston is ten miles away, but there's a small parade of shops at Pashton . . . a general store, chemist and a hairdresser. I'd give you a list of what would be required and where to get them.'

'Will Kira be here at those times?' I didn't like the idea of that broken man alone in the house.

She shrugged. 'She might be, but she doesn't normally look after Mr Race. However, you don't have to worry;

30

unless there's someone else here — me, my husband or one of the Engletons — we never leave him. There used to be a couple of young girls who came in from the village to care for Mr Race since I'm really the housekeeper, but they've gone off to university now, which is why you were employed.'

'Didn't Kira want to take their place?' I was being nosey, but I did wonder why Race's niece couldn't have stepped into the vacant position. She didn't appear to be permanently employed.

'I don't like to leave her with him for too long. I'm not sure I could trust her as a carer.'

While she was speaking about Kira I had felt an undercurrent of something but I couldn't quite place what it was. Had she found the girl's attitude towards her uncle as callous as I had?

'Also, she's a part-time assistant at the Library in Brancaster,' Mary went on. 'And anyway, I'm not sure how long those two are going to be at Great Haddows. She and her brother came over for their parents' funeral and have been here ever since. Mr Landon, the solicitor who manages everything, said they could stay while things were sorted out, so Wren transferred to his company's London office and commutes there most days. Kira seems to spend most of her time in Mr Race's library here going through old books and papers — she's bookish, I suppose.'

'Do you think they'll return to South Africa?'

Mary shrugged. 'I've no idea, but now they've seen Mr Race's condition is stabilised, I can't see why they wouldn't.'

Nor could I, and I was amused and annoyed in equal measure by the stab of disappointment I experienced. But even as I inwardly chastised myself for being so predictable — hero worship of the worst kind! — I realised that this was the first time I had thought about relationships since my father had first become ill. For that reason, I accepted it was a healthy sign. Not a realistic sign where Wren was concerned, of course, but it meant I was coming to terms with the changes in my life my parents' deaths had wrought.

I thought about Martin, the school friend who had grown to mean more, with whom I'd had so many fun times before my father became ill.

We had planned and expected our relationship to survive the three long years of attending separate universities, but in the end he went away while I stayed at home, and when he returned it was with someone else on his arm. Someone who wasn't tied at home.

That had hurt — more than I could share at the time as it would have distressed my father who would have blamed himself. So I held the pain to myself and swore that never again would I get involved with anyone. It was simply teenage angst running high, but circumstance had stepped in and made my sad resolve a reality — I hadn't had the time to meet other people.

Perhaps now I would have that opportunity.

* ★ ★ ★

That evening, after I had settled Race comfortably in bed, I chose to watch the TV in my own room. I was still getting used to the idea of living in someone else's house and wanted to spend some time alone. I became so engrossed in the programme I was following that it was a surprise to find it was after midnight.

Mary had prepared fish for supper which had been rather salty, and I found my mouth was dry as a bone. Pulling my cardigan more tightly round me — I had learned that the old house lost heat rapidly when the central heating went off in the evening — I slipped onto the landing and headed down the stairs to get a glass of water.

Voices came from the TV room which I would have ignored had I not heard my own name being mentioned.

'Jennie has no experience as a carer, so it would be easy to pull the wool over her eyes.'

I recognised Kira's distinctive South African accent. It felt like a slap in the face and what little confidence I had began draining out of me until I her heard her brother's reply.

'I wouldn't be so sure,' he said, 'she seemed pretty sharp to me.'

I was ridiculously pleased by his response, having been hurt by Kira's dismissal of me. It was true I had little professional experience, but I had been caring for people for a good few years and knew the correct way to do it.

I heard them move towards the door and hurried in the direction of the kitchen. I didn't want them to come into the hall and find me, for although I hadn't meant to eavesdrop they might not see it that way.

As I turned on the tap to fill my glass, Kira joined me.

'Did you bring the baby monitor with you?' she asked, referring to the intercom system Mary had shown me I should use to listen out for Race when he was alone.

'No, I've only been two minutes.' I sounded defensive, I knew.

She beheld me with those clear green eyes.

'A lot can happen in two minutes, you know.'

'Give the poor girl a break, Kira, she's been on duty all day.'

Wren had followed his sister from the den.

Kira gave him a strange, knowing look before turning on her heel and leaving.

'She doesn't mean anything,' he said, giving me one of those broad, winning smiles, 'It's just that she worries about Race.'

I determined I would not go weak at the knees and simper, but it took some effort. I nodded my thanks, returned his smile and padded off upstairs.

Wren was a real charmer, but I wasn't sure about his sister. It seemed she viewed me as naïve and even incompetent without ever having given me a chance, and that made all my old doubts about my ability as a paid carer rise up again.

Then I remembered my father's favourite quotation: *No one can make you feel inferior without your consent.*

'Who said that?' I'd asked him the first time I heard it.

'Eleanor Roosevelt, wife of the wartime president of the United States. Remember, darling girl, if the wife of the most powerful man in the world sometimes found people were trying to put her down, it's a sure bet the rest of us will experience something similar at some point in our lives. When it happens to you, take her advice and refuse to accept it.'

'I'll try.' And I had, though I learned it wasn't always easy to live up to her words.

I vowed I was not going to give Kira my consent. I needed this job and didn't want her turning her brother against me. Whatever she thought of me, I would prove her wrong!

2

Over the next few weeks I began to settle into my new life. Mary gradually showed me more and more of what I was expected to do, and as she much preferred housework to caring — she spent hours turning out cabinets, bookcases and cupboards — I tended to spend most of my time with Race.

Following Kira's comment, when I wasn't with him I made sure I always put the audio baby monitor in my pocket. That way I would always hear what was going on in his room, although in fact it was rare for him to do more than shift his position in his chair.

I learned that my working pattern would be six days on followed by three days off.

'You can borrow the car so you can get out of the valley if you want,' Mary said. 'There's not much to do in the village.'

This didn't surprise me. On the night I had arrived I had glimpsed a lone shop, dark and uninviting as the taxi sped past, and noticed the only pub in the area was boarded up with a *For Sale* sign outside.

The village was spread across the valley with odd cottages and farm buildings dotted about, but no real hamlet. Even the church stood alone and forlorn up an unmade road with a gloomy former rectory beside it. I could see why Mary thought I might want to get away.

'I'm around in the cottage most of the time when I'm off duty,' she explained, pointing towards the building next to the tennis court. 'My husband Brian is the gardener here, so if you want an evening off, that should be no problem. Mr Landon had the old stables converted after Mr Race became ill so there'd always be someone on site to see he was all right. It worked fine, too, until those two arrived.'

By *those two* I took her to mean Wren and Kira.

'Not that it isn't right that they should be here as Mr Race's next-of-kin,' she hurried on, as if anxious to prove she didn't disapprove of them. 'And it was very kind of them to insist I got extra help, even though my husband and I were managing very well with the girls from the village up until that point.'

I understood it then, Mary's lightly veiled animosity towards Wren and Kira. She saw their concern as interference — perhaps even criticism of the way she had arranged the care for their uncle — and had not welcomed my appointment.

I realised I would need to tread carefully or Mary would interpret any changes I might try to make as finding fault with her past practice. She had set up a streamlined operation and frowned upon any deviation from it.

The routine was, in fact, very

repetitious, but I soon realised that, whereas I might want to improve things for Mr Race, the way things were structured in the house made that difficult. Mary seemed to oversee everything and was constantly at my shoulder, checking up on me. The care she gave was professional but proprietorial, and I learned that any suggestion I might make was quickly dismissed.

So even though I discovered that whenever I returned from being off duty the TV was re-tuned to the cartoon channel, I realised there was nothing I could do. I wondered if Mary enjoyed watching them herself — it was plain Race wasn't interested — and I did feel rather aggrieved on his part that she would go for the lowest common denominator just because he was unwell.

'We've been living here for eight months ever since Mr Race became poorly,' she told me when I asked if he didn't have any friends who could visit. 'Things are running like clockwork. He becomes distressed by change and his old friends are distressed to see what he has become.'

I accepted what she said, although I wondered if seeing familiar faces wouldn't in fact help him. He might not have recognised his brother, but then he hadn't seen him for over twenty years. There was nothing to say he wouldn't know people with whom he had been in contact more recently. If we didn't try it, we'd never know.

It was an odd set-up. In spite of her possessive air, Mary's attitude towards her employer was correct but distant; she didn't seem to have any affection for Race. I knew carers had to keep professional boundaries in place but I wondered at her lack of warmth.

Still, she was the one with experience, and perhaps I was trying to get too close to him. I wished there was someone I could turn to for advice, but I didn't think Mrs Miller at the agency would be much help. She had found me the job and there her duty ended. And I didn't want to show my inexperience to

Wren and Kira by asking them either.

It appeared Mary hadn't much time for the people who lived in the far-flung village.

'They're a nosey lot,' she told me when I asked about the neighbours. 'And Mr Landon likes us to keep ourselves to ourselves. He and the doctor think it would be unfair to encourage locals to gawp at Mr Race in his condition.'

'Were none of them his friends before he became ill?'

Mary gave me a pitying look. 'Mr Race and his wife were well out of the locals' league,' she sniffed. 'They ran a number of successful businesses from Great Haddows and were very wealthy. They enjoyed living in the country but had nothing in common with the other residents.'

'Oh, I hadn't realised you knew his wife.' Hadn't Mary just told me she and her husband had only moved in after his illness?

She managed to look uncomfortable and annoyed at the same time.

'Mr Landon told me,' was all she said, and her tone indicated the matter was closed.

★   ★   ★

Help came where I least expected it.

Although my shift pattern suited me very well, it did mean I was going a bit stir crazy by the sixth day, so was always pleased when Mary sent me off in the car on errands to the nearest town.

I longed for the opportunity to go walking other than around the garden, lovely as it was, but Mary was not keen for me to leave the property except by car, not even to venture into the wilderness beyond the formal, landscaped grounds.

'You don't want to be stopped by locals and subjected to an inquisition about Mr Race,' she insisted. 'Far better you drive to the country park just outside Dawston and walk around there.'

However I was from a country village myself and missed the camaraderie one so often finds in small, self-sufficient communities — and yes, I'll admit, I missed the friendly banter and the gossip as well. Whereas Wren was all amiable pleasantness, he was not often around, and his brief interactions with me could not make up for Mary's distant formality and Kira's watchfulness — and I saw a lot more of them.

As for Mary's husband, I had only glimpsed him in the garden — a giant of a man with huge shoulders and a boxer's misshapen nose, both attributes giving him a somewhat frightening appearance which made me disinclined to seek him out to start up a conversation.

So once I had given Race his lunch and walked him along the upstairs corridor, I took to going for a brisk walk around the gardens.

I tried to remember to take my phone with me as I had given Mary my number so she could call if she needed me, but I often forgot. I did wonder if deep down in my subconscious I did so on purpose. Nature soothed my soul, and who wanted to be interrupted by a ringtone then? My spirits always rose when communing with nature, and I enjoyed exploring the beautiful grounds that surrounded the house.

They showed the hand of a real plantsman, and I exclaimed again and again as I came upon ever more rare and beautiful plants just bursting into bud. I wondered who had planned the design, for it was a mature landscape and, as the Kents had only been at Great Haddows for a year, it couldn't have been Brian.

Striding along the path to the distant fields, my eyes glued on the sheets of snowdrops sheltering around the bowls of the trees, I catapulted straight into a man staring up at an old apple tree.

'Excuse me!' he exclaimed, even though it was clearly my mistake.

I found myself staring up at a friendly, questioning face.

'I'm so sorry,' I said, 'I wasn't looking where I was going.'

'No,' he agreed, 'You seemed to be on an important mission!'

I laughed, his good humour cutting across my embarrassment.

'Sometimes I have a desperate need to be outside,' I said. 'And once I get there I tend to forget about everything but my surroundings.'

'The great outdoors does clear the mind,' he agreed. 'When I've been cooped up indoors too long I have to pace quickly, then I feel free again!'

He understood! It was as if two like souls had come together. Being outside always spoke to me of freedom and confined spaces terrified me.

'I'm Mr Race's new carer,' I introduced myself. 'Who are you?'

'Doug Edwards.'

He held out his hand, and I shook it.

He reminded me of someone, but I couldn't think who. His hands were large and capable, and with his lantern jaw and rough broad shoulders he looked a typical countryman, personifying reliability in the way that someone with Wren's amazing bones and charisma could not.

'Mr Kent — Brian — often calls me

in to do specialist work in the garden.'

He pointed to a van just visible beyond the bare beech hedge. *Douglas Edwards*, I read, *Tree Surgeon and Landscape Garden Designer — no job too small.* This was followed by an address in Dawston and a local phone number.

'I often do work here,' he continued. 'Brian called me in to look at this old girl.' He patted the gnarled trunk in front of him. 'It's riddled with canker and is too big to spray. She'll have to come down if we're to protect the younger trees.'

'I'm Jennie Wright. I'm here caring for Mr Race,' I repeated.

'Yes, Brian told me. What a relief for Mary — she's done so much for Mr Race up until now. Brian is a gardener, and caring isn't his forte. It must be such a help to have you on hand.'

There was something about this cheerful, ordinary man that told me I could let down my guard. In the house I felt as if I was acting a part — being the competent, controlled carer — unable to approach Mary or Kira for fear of appearing unable to do the job, but I badly needed to talk to someone.

'I don't know that it is — a relief, I mean. Mary doesn't seem very happy that I'm here.'

'What do you mean?' He cocked his head on one side, inviting me to explain.

'Well, there are things I'd like to do which I think she'd disapprove of, though I'm sure they would be good for Mr Race.'

'Like what?'

His easy manner was reassuring, so I told him about the tight regime which kept Race marooned upstairs and the way Mary seemed not to notice this was bad for him. I mentioned my feeling that while very competent, she didn't actually seem very fond of him, and I also noted that Kira seemed unfriendly.

In fact, I said far too much.

I needn't have worried — Doug proved to be the perfect listener.

'It's only natural you should worry about Mr Race — it's your job, after all,' he said. 'But I wonder if you aren't imagining things? Brian says Kira is a spoiled madam who looks for things to complain about, so what you're interpreting as disapproval is probably just her normal nature. And perhaps Mary keeps her distance from Mr Race to protect herself. I would think it must be hard to get close to someone you're caring for and then to lose them, don't you find that?'

He asked me as if I'd had that experience. I hadn't professionally, of course, but I had with my parents. It hadn't struck me that Mary could be fearful of being hurt in a similar fashion, but I realised it was probably the truth. After all, on hearing that I was taking this job, the bereavement counsellor had stressed that I should maintain professional boundaries to protect myself from just such an eventuality.

'You need to get out more yourself,' Doug went on. 'There's a barn dance at the village hall a week on Saturday, in aid of the renovation of the church spire. Would you like to come?'

I was due to be off-duty that weekend. It was ages since I had been asked out and thought what fun it would be to have some relaxation.

'I'd love to,' I replied.

Yet as we parted company and I headed out towards the field, I began to have doubts.

Mary had been so insistent I shouldn't talk about the family to any locals — would she place Dawston, the nearest town, into that category?

I hoped I hadn't said too much. Perhaps Doug was a great friend of Brian's and wouldn't like me suggesting his wife was somehow lacking in care.

★   ★   ★

I felt even worse about what I had said when two days later I reported to Mary that the cold Race had been fighting had moved onto his chest and he appeared to be having trouble breathing. Her concern was palpable, and once she had checked on his condition she was clearly very worried indeed.

'I'll phone the doctor,' she said, and later I heard her describing Race's symptoms to him and insisting he needed a home visit at once.

'If he dies it will be the end of everything!'

Her voice was high pitched with emotion, and I felt ashamed as I realised how wrong I had been and how very much she did care.

Dr Carlton arrived two hours later.

He was a big, florid man, with wild hair and an unctuous manner. I didn't take to him, especially when he dismissed my gentle suggestion that Race wasn't being stimulated enough.

'My dear young lady,' he said, fixing me with a patronising gaze, 'Mr Engleton couldn't cope with stimulation. He needs to be kept calm and rested. If you have been trying to force him to engage with you it could be why he has developed this chest infection.'

Even I knew bacteria rather than

stimulation caused infection!

I met his eyes and refused to drop my own, and eventually he turned away.

Luckily Mary wasn't in the room to hear what he had said. I rather feared she was the type of person who would be overawed by the doctor's credentials and believe him.

No wonder Race wasn't doing very well if he had Dr Carlton for a GP. Only, I later discovered, he didn't.

'Dr Carlton is a private doctor from London,' Mary explained when he had gone. 'Mr Landon said we needed continuity of care and you can't guarantee seeing the same doctor in a GP practice these days.'

I thought I would rather be seen by a dozen different competent GPs than the smarmy Dr Carlton! But I said nothing. It seemed the rich were different — they wanted a tame doctor always on call.

Before he came I had meant to ask him about taking Race outside, but now I was glad I hadn't. I was sure he would repeat what Mary had told me he had said previously and insist it would harm him. However, now that I knew Dr Carlton wasn't so much protective as controlling, I felt absolved from any of his instructions.

I had maligned poor Mary, accusing her of having no feelings for Race. Clearly, she was just following the doctor's orders, being of an age that was more deferential to medics, whereas I judged them on results.

I remembered the doctors who had treated my father, and then my mother. They had been keen for my parents to retain as good a quality of life as they could for as long as possible, yet it appeared Race's doctor encouraged his impoverished lifestyle. It was surprising, but I had merely smiled at him when he insisted Race should be kept calm and determined that I would have to try and improve my employer's day by stealth.

I wondered what Wren and Kira thought about their uncle's medical care and decided to broach the subject with them.

'Dr Carlton came to see Race today,' I said to Wren that evening when we were temporarily alone in the lounge. Mary was on an evening off and had prepared a meat pie for us which Kira had heated up. 'Have you met him?'

'Yes, he spoke to Kira and me when we first arrived and explained the situation with Race, but we were still in shock over our parents' deaths, so I don't remember much of what he said.'

That figured. All my instincts told me that Wren was a good man who would want the best for his uncle, but if he was unaware of the constraints being put upon Race, he would have no reason to question the doctor's treatment.

'I — I thought it might be good for your uncle if he went out more.' I knew I couldn't complain about Dr Carlton, all I had was a faint feeling of disquiet about the way he did things, and who was I — an unqualified carer — to question him? But I wanted to ascertain just what Wren thought about my plan.

'Did Dr Carlton agree?'

'No,' I had to admit, 'he felt it would be too much for him.'

'Are you sure he's not right — might Race deteriorate if he goes outside?'

I threw caution to the wind.

'I think Dr Carlton's insistence that your uncle stays indoors is more about his own fear that he might be sued if Race fell over and broke a hip, rather than concern about his patient's well-being. Otherwise I can't see why a medical man should be so risk averse.'

Wren stared at me and seemed to be considering what I had said. I felt uncomfortable under such scrutiny. Finally he broke the silence.

'I don't think you should do anything unless you are certain it's safe.'

His answer didn't really tell me what he thought, but it was ambiguous enough to give me leeway.

'I won't,' I agreed, already sure that what I planned would not harm Race.

He gave me one of his blinding smiles.

'No, I don't believe you ever would. You clearly like my uncle and want to protect him. How are you finding living here? Isn't it a bit lonely?'

I smiled back — it was impossible not to. Wren's charm was infectious and his very presence encouraged you to relax and let his bonhomie wash over you.

'I'm used to being on my own and there are more people at Great Haddows than there were when I was at home with my mother.'

'But don't you want to go out sometimes?'

'Yes, of course, and I will. I want to explore the church and the local shop, and I'll borrow the car sometime and go further afield.'

Though in fact I had no idea where I would head for.

'Well, there's great excitement in the village next week — a barn dance, no less. How about coming with Kira and me?'

'Actually . . . I'm already going,' I said.

'With whom?'

Kira's voice was sharp as she joined us, and I wondered how long she had been standing by the door listening to our conversation.

'With Doug Edwards, the tree surgeon.'

'Oh, yes, you know him, Wren — the guy who seems to spend an inordinate amount of time at Great Haddows without actually doing much.'

'He's going to cut down the infected apple tree,' I retorted, stung on Doug's behalf. I didn't see Kira doing much about the place!

'Well, that should be interesting to see,' Wren joined in. 'As Kira said, Doug's here quite a lot and yet few trees seem to receive his attention.'

I thought I ought to defend my new friend, but then saw the look the siblings exchanged and decided discretion was the better part of valour.

'I'm going upstairs to write a letter to my parents' old neighbour,' I said by way of excuse for leaving. 'Goodnight.'

As I climbed the stairs, Kira's voice drifted up.

'Pretty interesting that Doug has invited her, don't you think?'

But I couldn't hear Wren's response.

Truth to tell I would have loved to be going to the dance with him; the image of our arms entwined as we bobbed and galloped and do-si-doed was enticing, but by including Kira in his invitation he had made it clear this was merely him being polite and it should not be considered a date.

* * *

Once in my room I sat down at the dressing table with my writing case and started to write.

Jean Kerr had lived in the cottage next door to ours and had supported me all she could during the last dark years at home.

I say *all she could* because Jean was riddled with arthritis, and had been since my parents had first moved into the village, so *they* had taken to helping *her* manage by doing her shopping, giving her lifts and undertaking simple DIY tasks.

In return she had become my honorary grandmother and confidante, to whom I had turned when I needed advice outside the family, and this had continued when I'd had to take over the tasks for her that up until then had been performed for her by Mum and Dad.

Finally, I began to write . . .

Dear Jean

How are you? I hope your new neighbours are nice. I miss you and our little chats, but hopefully I'll be able to pop up to see you in a month or two.

Well, I've been here some weeks now, and I'm beginning to learn the ropes. Mr Engleton is a sad case — his illness had left him quite disabled. He doesn't seem able to recognise anything or anyone around him, though I wonder if that's because he sees no one he used to know. Mary, his housekeeper, me, and even his niece and nephew are all new to him since he became ill.

I had hoped to test this theory, but his doctor doesn't want him to be over-stimulated and the housekeeper, Mary, follows his orders to the letter! I can understand why — she's devoted to Mr Engleton although she keeps it well hidden. I'd originally thought she was cold towards him but it turns out she's just protecting herself from being hurt. She was distraught when she thought he might be dying! Anyway, she doesn't question Dr Carlton's instructions. But since I do, it may put us on a collision course eventually! At the moment I'm being very cautious, but if she finds out what I am tentatively trying to do, there are likely to be eruptions.

Kira and Wren Engleton are my client's nephew and niece, who came to England six months ago when their parents, Paul and Nola, died in a car crash. They've been here ever since.

I haven't made my mind up about them yet. She's a beauty and he really deserves the title 'drop dead gorgeous', but I'm not sure what they're really like. He seems to be very friendly and kind, but his sister is rather sharp and watches everything I do as if looking to catch me out. Hopefully, I won't do anything to incur her wrath, but it does feel uncomfortable.

And that's the rub, really. Living in someone else's house is not as easy as having my own place. It's as if I have to be on my guard the whole time and can't let my defences down. It's not the Engletons' fault or even Mary's, it's just I feel I always need to be on my best behaviour. In fact, the only time I can relax is when I'm alone with Mr Engleton — he's called Race, by the way — because *he doesn't judge me.*

I shouldn't complain, though. I've got a lovely room of my own in a beautiful house, and in spite of her devotion to Dr Carlton's regime, Mary does leave me pretty much to my own devices. She sees her role more as the housekeeper — she's red hot on tidying and knowing where everything is which is just as well in this house of nooks and crannies! So I'm free to do the caring as long as I stick to her rules! And I'm being well paid for what I do.

I know I have to accept my current situation because it's the first step towards a new life, whatever I decide that will be. And no one is being unkind to me — it's just there are constraints living in someone else's house.

Haddows is a straggling village which covers a large area but doesn't seem to have a heart. There's a shop and a church, but that's it. Apparently the Engletons have lived here for generations, so they must have made their own entertainment in years gone by. Still, there's a barn dance next week, and I'm going with a chap I've met, and hopefully I'll meet some more people there.

So don't worry about me, I know I made the right decision in coming here. It's a really good opportunity for me to get on my feet, and I'm only sounding off to you because I need to get things off my chest and I know you'll understand.

Much love, Jennie xxx

I put down my pen and read over what I had written. The last paragraph said it all, really, and I wasn't just trying to put Jean's mind at ease. My situation could be so much worse and I really did have nothing to complain about.

Yet still I had to acknowledge to myself that every so often I got the oddest feeling that somehow things weren't quite right. I couldn't put my finger on it or explain it, and could only assume that living in someone else's house had that effect on me.

It wasn't the end of the world but it was disquieting, and I hoped that once I had really settled in the feeling would pass. At that point in time I truly believed I could be happy at Great Haddows.

How little I knew then!

3

Knowing I was going to the barn dance in a few days, I turned my attention to what I might wear. I knew it wouldn't be a dressy occasion, but my wardrobe was very limited anyway.

Although I had been able to take a few temporary jobs while nursing my parents, it hadn't been possible to work full-time so I hadn't much money to spend on clothes. I decided that now I was earning I would buy something new.

On my next day off, I borrowed the car and drove into Dawston, the nearest town, intent on enjoying some retail therapy, something of which I had little experience!

Dawston did not have a huge choice, but it was enough for me. I avoided the boutiques where the clothes in the window had no prices — even I knew that if you had to ask you couldn't afford it! I concentrated on the two cut-price outlets on the high street. I enjoyed trying on various outfits, and eventually chose a red circle skirt, reminiscent of those vintage fifties fashions you see flaring out in old rock'n'roll movies as the stars jive the night away. I hoped mine would swing around me in a similar way, trying to convince myself it was because I didn't want to appear out of place, while knowing deep down that there was another reason entirely that I wanted to look good.

* * *

When I arrived back at Great Haddows, Mary was sitting at the kitchen table.

'Jane is upstairs,' she said.

Jane was Race's personal trainer. I have perhaps given the impression that no one else in the house thought it worthwhile to try and improve Race's situation, but that was not strictly true.

When I shared my plan with her, Jane said she thought it would be an excellent idea to take him outside, and told me how often I should walk him along the corridor and that I should get him to stand up out of his chair frequently to strengthen his muscles ready for the adventure.

'His walking has definitely improved,' she said as she put him through his paces on her last visit. 'I told Mary that he could do with seeing a physiotherapist regularly, but she said the doctor wasn't keen.'

'That doesn't surprise me!' I simply couldn't contain myself.

She'd nodded. 'He does seem to believe in masterly inactivity. Anyway, if you do take Race outside you'll need help to get him up and down the stairs. I wouldn't want you trying alone, it wouldn't be safe.'

I had been thinking this myself. It was one thing to support Race on the flat, but it would take two of us if we wanted to get him at ground level.

I knew Jane wouldn't be able to assist because her appointments were only half an hour long and it would take all that time just to get Race outside, let alone go for a walk and then return upstairs.

I wondered who else might help me — I knew Mary wouldn't approve, so she was out, and I doubted Kira would want to, given her outburst about the pathos of her uncle's life. Then there was Wren — but he had not seemed too keen on the idea when I had spoken to him about it.

What I really needed was someone who would be happy to lend a hand without questioning me about risks and safety and advisability. If Race was getting better — and Jane had said he was and that walking outside could help him — I knew I simply had to find an answer.

It was late closing at the library that evening, so Kira wouldn't be home until after nine. Wren got home from work at six, and catching him alone, I decided to have another go.

'Jane was here earlier.'

We were in the sitting-room and I bent down to replace a magazine I had been reading in the fine antique Canterbury the family used for periodicals. With my back to him I found it easier to say what I wanted.

'The personal trainer, you know?'

He said nothing, so I took a deep breath and continued, 'She thinks Race is improving and that going out in the garden for a walk would be good for him. I wondered if you would be willing to help me bring him downstairs tomorrow?'

Even though it was my day off, I had agreed to stand in for Mary for an hour the next day while she went into town to collect a parcel from the sorting office that the postman had been unable to deliver. I thought that would give me ample time to carry out my plan.

Silence from behind me.

Then, just when I thought he

couldn't have heard, he said, 'I have to go to London tomorrow.'

'On a Saturday?'

Wren usually only worked Monday to Friday.

'Oh, it's not work. Kira and I have an appointment with someone.'

'So you'll miss the barn dance?'

My heart sank, and I realised it wasn't just the thought of him not being able to assist me with Race that disappointed me.

'No, we'll definitely be back in time,' he said. 'They're going to be serving craft ale at the bar, and I've developed a real taste for your specialist English beers.'

Why on earth did I feel relieved when he said that? What was it to me if he was there or not? It was Doug who would be partnering me. But still, the news did seem to make the world brighter.

★ ★ ★

The following evening Doug called for me at seven o'clock. Kira let him in as I was putting the finishing touches to my make-up, which meant I was just descending the stairs as they walked from the front door.

'You look amazing!' Doug's face lit up, and I was vain enough to be pleased I had made the right choice in the outfit department. Kira raised an eyebrow and gave a little smile. She seemed to know something I didn't.

'You will go to the ball, Cinderella,' she said, at the same time waving a pretend wand. 'Or do I mean to the church?'

'The church?'

She laughed. 'Haven't you told her, Doug?' She turned back to me. 'You'll be dancing in the aisles! The village hall is in the church!'

'What do you mean?'

'St Cyprian's, that huge gothic edifice just back from the main road, was built to replace a smaller Norman church which was in fact a much better sized

72

place for such a sprawling parish. Haddows has always been a large farming village where houses are few and far between, so there never was much of a congregation. But you know the Victorians! Anyway, about five years ago it was touch and go whether the church would have to close as the cost of its upkeep was just too great. Then the parochial church council came up with the idea that if half of the building was made into a village hall — which Haddows had never had and had always wanted — the other half could continue as the church . . . and that's what's happened.'

'You know a lot about the area for someone from South Africa,' Doug said. He had been watching her carefully.

Kira tilted her head and returned his gaze.

'The local history centre shares premises with the library, so I have lots of time to read up about Haddows — its houses, its heroes and villains, and all the nefarious goings on since time immemorial!' She appeared to be teasing him.

'Interesting,' said Doug.

But when we had closed the front door behind us he let his true feelings out. 'I've only met her a couple of times when I've been doing work at Great Haddows, but I find her a bit strange — she works part-time yet doesn't seem to do much. I don't know why she and her brother don't just go home — they've been here for months.'

It appeared I wasn't the only one who didn't feel entirely at ease with Race's niece, though I definitely wasn't itching for them to leave. Doug's words unsettled me and I refused to let myself consider why.

He led me out to his car — a very much more expensive model than I would have expected.

'This is nice.'

'Yes, I like it,' was all he said as he held the passenger door open.

When we arrived at St Cyprian's

there were already a lot of people there. I was interested to see that the 'village hall' had actually been an aisle to one side of the main church that was now shut off and a completely separate entity with a kitchen and small stage.

People were milling around the serving area, and a four-piece band was setting up on the stage. The caller was dressed in jeans and a blue gingham shirt with a shoestring necktie of braided leather secured with an ornamental clasp. On his head he wore a Stetson, his cowboy boots completing the picture. He certainly looked the part.

'I hadn't realised there were so many people living in Haddows,' I said as Doug handed me a glass of white wine.

He laughed. 'There aren't. Barry Creer, the caller, and his band are very popular, so this lot will have come from all over.'

'Do you know many of them — I mean, have you lived here long?'

He took a sip of his wine and

regarded me quizzically. 'What's with all the questions?' He asked. 'You're a right little inquisitor, aren't you?'

'I don't mean to be,' I said, embarrassed. 'It's just it's difficult to know what to talk about when you've only just met someone.'

Fortunately, at that moment the band struck up and Barry urged us all to get onto the dance floor, so the awkward situation passed.

'Come on!'

Doug grabbed my hand and pulled me forwards, barely giving me time to set down my glass.

I've always loved dancing. I used to go to ballet lessons when I was young, and whereas I was never in line to be a ballerina, I still really enjoyed social dancing. Movement to music spoke to my soul, and I was soon swinging happily to the beat, obeying the caller's instructions:

'Bow to your partner . . . your corners all . . . join hands in a circle . . . skip round the hall . . . '

We skipped.

'Hand over hand, around you go . . . when you meet your partner say hello . . . turn around and go the other way . . . '

The members of our set came in all shapes and sizes and as we danced I played a game in my mind categorising them — probably quite incorrectly.

Those towering men were farmers and their plump partners their wives; arty types with wispy beards were teachers; giggling girls wearing inappropriate shoes worked in offices; the laughing grey-haired couple were silver surfers remembering their youth; while the older women who watched the behaviour of others with beady eyes were stern but respected matriarchs.

The great thing was that no one was left out and all were enjoying themselves. That's what I loved about barn dances — or was it square dancing? I was never sure of the difference — that everyone was included. I wondered if Race would have come, had he been in good health — even now, he could have joined the older contingent who were sitting gossiping on the side-lines as the rest of us galloped by.

'Turn your partner right hand around . . . promenade around as if you're bound . . . '

Doug was a good partner, and we made a pretty decent pair as we hand-over-handed and stripped the willow. My skirt flared out and my ponytail bounced, and I realised I hadn't had so much fun since before my parents died.

'Come back home and swing your own . . . '

Doug slipped his left arm round my back to meet my right one as I crossed it over my chest.

'Bal-ance and swing and sway . . . '

I swung, and as I turned, I caught sight of Wren, standing by the bar, watching.

I almost lost my step but managed to get back on the right foot and continue in the foursome right-handed star. Yet my mind was racing. Why had he been staring at me? Did it mean he liked what he saw? Had my skirt fanned out prettily as I turned? Or in my exertions, was my face red and blotchy? And why should I care?

It was a question I didn't want to consider, so I forced my attention back to the dance. Doug hadn't seemed to have noticed my confusion, and I took his outstretched arm to split to the centre to a line of four.

Finally the music ended and the floor erupted into applause and laughter. Doug led me back to the bar where I asked for a glass of water to slake my thirst. I needed to sit the next dance out to catch my breath, and collapsed thankfully on one of the hard chairs at the side of the room.

Doug's phone rang and he, having registered who was calling him, excused himself to go and answer it.

'Can't hear myself think in here!' he joked, and I nodded my agreement.

I turned to watch the swirling patterns the dancers were making on the floor. There was something so infectious about folk music, and my feet were tapping away in unison.

Out of the corner of my eye I saw Wren and Kira, promenading together. They made a handsome couple and both were light on their feet. I noted that many of the girls standing on the sidelines were ogling Wren, and I realised how ridiculous I was in being one of their number. How could I be so shallow as to be moved by just good looks? But I knew that I was. I consoled myself that perhaps that was what women like me were meant to do — be attracted to the most attractive, while also accepting that we were unlikely to get the prize. Wren set my pulses racing, yet I never felt fully at ease in his company. Why was that? I supposed that it might be because, like Mary had said about Race and his neighbours, he was out of my league.

The thought so disturbed me that I got up and wandered outside. The cool evening air was a relief after the frenzied heat in the hall, and I walked towards the lych-gate.

'She doesn't know anything.' I heard Doug's voice before I saw him. 'You don't have to worry.'

'Doug?'

He stepped out from behind the cedar tree near the boundary wall.

'Got to go now,' he told his caller, before coming to join me. 'My aunt.' He indicated his mobile phone. 'She's concerned about her daughter's birthday present. She wants it to be a big secret.'

He smiled, and I told myself what a very nice man he was. It was true he didn't have the charm and charisma of Wren, but that was almost a relief as he was so straightforward and didn't play games — which I suspected Wren did.

I decided it must be quite wearying to be seen out and about with a stunner like Kira's brother — I could imagine everyone wondering what an attractive man was doing with an ordinary girl, a girl . . . well, a girl like me.

Not that there would ever be a chance of that.

I was, after all, very average, and Wren could expect the best.

Thank heavens for Doug's normality. He was pleasant in both looks and manner, but not so outstanding as to be intimidating. We were probably well-suited, so why did I find that thought slightly depressing?

'Doug, I wonder if you'd help me?' I needed to break away from my thoughts. 'I think I told you that I want to improve Race's life? Well, I was wondering if you would help me during the week to bring him downstairs so he can walk in the garden? The weather is warming up and the fresh air would do him the power of good, but I can't manage it alone.'

He stopped to consider my request.

'I'll have to see what I can do.'

I would have liked to tie him down to committing to a day and time when Mary would be out, but just then the emergency doors crashed open and a crowd of young people poured out to cool off.

'Looks like there'll be more room on the dance-floor now. Let's go back in.' And he took my hand and pulled me inside.

The music was still going strong, and I marvelled at the pace of the fiddle.

'Once and half around you go . . . '

I allowed myself to be led onto the floor.

'When you meet this time, turn back again . . . '

I laced hands with the others in the set, travelling from right to left and then returning.

'Now, swing . . . as if this partner is your own . . . call her darling, call her dear . . . and waltz with her if it takes all year.'

It was a shock to find myself in Wren's arms!

I didn't think he had been in our set originally, but suddenly there he was, holding me close and whirling me round the room. My chest felt as if it was bursting and my heart was beating out a tattoo so loudly I was sure he must be able to hear it over the music. This was so different from partnering Doug — this time, every bone in my body was melting as he held me in his arms and I was willing the dance never to end.

I gasped as we galloped past Kira and Doug, now partnering each other. He looking thunderously in our direction; she with an amused smile.

At last the music stopped, and Wren let me go.

'Thank you.' I tried to be blasé, but I suspected my behaviour had been all too obvious. His touch had made me come alive!

'I enjoyed it, too.' He took my hand and gave it a gallant, continental kiss. I felt like a Ruritanian princess.

'We lost each other.' Doug glowered as he marched towards us. 'Don't know how it happened.' But he gave Wren a look which clearly said differently.

'Blame me.' Kira was coming up

behind him. 'I have absolutely no sense of rhythm and ended up crashing into your set. Wren tried to guide me back, but I'm afraid I'm a lady who won't be led — I like to lead myself!'

The brilliant smile she flashed him seemed to soothe Doug, though I wasn't sure if he believed her. I didn't. It had seemed to me to be a very calculated encounter, and if Kira had been part of the ambush, then so too had Wren, for she had not acted alone.

Why should they have engineered it — what purpose had it served except to annoy Doug? This was all getting far too complicated for me!

'Doug, would you get me a drink, please?' Kira drew him away from us, and I couldn't help but feel that she had a reason for doing so. But what? Did she fancy Doug? It seemed far-fetched but maybe that was the answer.

Seeing my confusion Wren hurried to reassure me. 'Don't worry, she just wants to talk to him for a bit,' he said. 'She'll give him back later.'

'I see.' I felt such a fool.

So Wren had only changed partners to enable his sister to get close to Doug. Well, what had I expected — that he might actually want to dance with me?

'I'm sorry you had to suffer my dancing to ensure she could,' I offered.

His green eyes looked amused. 'Oh, I didn't suffer at all, in fact I wanted to dance with you. You created quite a stir in your circular skirt — a real *Lady In Red.*'

I blushed, not sure whether to be flattered or embarrassed. I had wanted to look good, but not to be overly conspicuous. 'I like red,' was all I could think of to say.

'And it certainly likes you!' He smiled and kissed my hand again. My stomach lurched as I felt the tension in the air. 'So how are you finding your job, Jennie Wright? Is it turning out as you expected?'

'Pretty much.' I knew my voice sounded squeaky and I wished I could control it. 'I needed a live-in post to get back on my feet, and that's exactly what I'm doing. I do feel sorry for Race, though. I wish he could enjoy life more.'

'As I understand it he enjoyed life to the full before he became ill.' Wren sounded somewhat unsympathetic, I thought. 'Perhaps this is the price you pay for over-indulging.'

'Did he? Over-indulge, I mean?'

'Apparently so — he appears to have been quite a lad in his day.'

'Even so, no one deserves what has happened to him.'

He indicated his agreement with a slight nod. 'You're right, but I wonder if his present situation is a result of his excesses in the past.'

'I hope I'm not judged on my past transgressions.'

'I'm not suggesting people should be, and anyway, I can't believe you have many.'

I wanted to change the subject.

'Was your father like Race?'

'Not at all — Dad was straight as a

die. That's why they became estranged, I think. And I don't believe they would have got together again if Race hadn't written to him after Aunt Susan died.'

'But you said he didn't recognise your father?'

'No, he didn't — it was too late. Maybe he would have remembered something if he and Mum had been around longer, but they died three weeks after arriving here. A double tragedy.'

'I'm so sorry.'

'It was hard, but life goes on.'

I steeled myself for what I said next. 'I'm surprised you've stayed so long at Great Haddows. Don't you miss your home?'

'In South Africa, you mean?' I nodded and he went on, 'We need to sort things out here before we can return.'

'You mean you think Race may come to understand who you are?'

'No, I don't hold out any hope there — he's a very sick man. But Dad was concerned about him so I want to make sure he's OK before we go.'

I wanted to ask him what he was concerned about, but Doug and Kira returned from their talk so there was no opportunity to do so.

The band struck up again after their break, and Doug led me onto the dance floor in a very determined fashion.

'Now everybody swing, swing . . . ' called Barry Creer, still going strong.

Only it wasn't the same. The sheer fun of it had gone for me now I'd experienced the overwhelming excitement of waltzing with Wren. Oh, I whooped and dived with the best of them and tried hard to hide the way I was feeling, and I think I achieved my goal, as Doug didn't complain, but deep inside I knew that something was missing.

As I've explained, I'm the original scaredy-cat, so I didn't dare explore what it was or why I felt that way, because I knew it would be dangerous.

Doug drove me back to Great Haddows, and I was pleased he didn't try to cuddle me in the car. However, when he helped me out of my seat he pulled me to him and planted a kiss on my lips. I didn't feel I could resist, guilt at my reaction to Wren's attention clouding my judgment.

'Goodnight, Jennie. I hope we'll do this again.'

'Thank you for a lovely evening.' I didn't commit to more and turned on my heel for the front door.

Kira and Wren had just beaten me home and clearly had seen our embrace.

'You enjoyed yourself, I see.' Kira was her usual brittle self.

'Which is a good thing and not surprising.' Wren was more amenable. 'I enjoyed myself.'

For a moment our eyes met and I felt again that crackle of excitement like when we had danced.

I knew I had to get away. I turned and fled upstairs, Kira's laughter ringing in my ears.

I didn't think so fondly of Wren two days later, when Mary called me into the kitchen and read me the riot act.

'What's all this about you trying to get others to help you take Mr Race outside?' she demanded. 'I thought Dr Carlton had made it quite clear that such exertion would be too much for him and we need to keep him calm at all times.'

'Jane and I think it might help him and — '

'And is either one of you a doctor? No, I thought not! You are here to carry out the doctor's orders, not to make up your own. If you can't manage that you're welcome to leave!'

Her threat pulled me up short. If I lost this job I had nowhere to go, which was worrying, but even more concerning was the thought that if I left, Race would have no one in his corner.

I had thought that Wren was determined to ensure his uncle was OK, but clearly I had been wrong. It could only have been he who told Mary of my intentions, knowing that would scupper any chance of Race going outside and enjoying a slightly less restricted life.

I was hugely disappointed in Wren. I had thought he was a decent bloke, but this behaviour showed he wasn't. He hadn't even had the courtesy to tell me he disapproved of my intention, but rather had run straight to Mary to tell tales. Still, there was nothing I could do but give Mary my word I wouldn't change Race's routine.

I was pretty upset following this showdown and wondered how to react when I next saw Wren and Kira. I was sure she must have known what was going on all the time, witness the strange looks she gave me. I knew I was not her most favourite person.

Added to my misery and anger was the shaming knowledge that I had let myself go with Wren. I had been buzzing with adrenaline and hormones when he held me close, and my treacherous body had openly enjoyed the closeness of his. And when he'd kissed my hand I'd been transported to a fairytale land where dreams could come true! Now I felt humiliated and foolish — and my much-treasured belief that I was a good judge of character was broken.

Nevertheless, I realised that if I were to stay I had to face the brother and sister and not let them learn what I was thinking. I hadn't seen them before they left for work that morning, but I knew I would have to do so that evening and rather dreaded the experience.

* * *

After helping Race to shower I went back downstairs to find Mary sitting at the kitchen table. It was her day off and it was plain she was in a quandary. She didn't really trust me alone with Race for a whole day — even when off-duty she or her husband would be somewhere on the estate — and she was still annoyed with me, so didn't want to ask a favour of me. But as she let me know, she and Brian had been summoned to an urgent all-day appointment, and she had no choice. Having made it very clear I was not to change anything in her absence she left me on my own. I was rather surprised that she did.

I knew Doug was coming to remove the old apple tree that day, and when she had gone I thought what a shame it was that I had been forbidden to take Race out, as I could've asked him to help me while Mary and Brian were out of the way.

Doug arrived with his apprentice at ten o'clock. I made them both a cup of coffee, but we didn't have time to chat. He was working flat out, wanting to clear everything in the one day, and I was busy carrying out the household duties usually undertaken by Mary.

By six o'clock I was not only tired but also on edge at the thought of eating dinner with Wren. It was late opening at the library which meant Kira wouldn't be back until nine, so when I heard the front door open it could only be her brother, and I waited until he wandered into the kitchen.

I took a deep breath and said, 'Hello.'

'Hello.' He was neither friendly nor unfriendly. 'What's for supper?'

'Mary had to go out, but she left some steak and kidney, so I've made a pudding with potatoes and greens,' I explained.

I was all too aware of how close he was standing and of his intense gaze. I wanted to dislike him but even now that I knew how he had dropped me in it, my weak body still reacted to him.

'I'll leave a plate meal out for Kira to heat up in the microwave when she gets in,' I added.

'Sounds wonderful,' he said. 'But you don't have to wait on us, you know. I'd have been just as happy with bread and cheese.'

'I had to prepare a meal for Race.' I felt his response was meant to be a thank you, though I found it rather a back-handed one.

'Are you OK?' Wren moved in front of the Aga and was now facing me. 'You seem different.'

'I'm fine.'

My response was a little too sharp, but think I managed to hide it by giving him a dazzling smile that I didn't feel. He had a curious expression on his face, but he said nothing.

It was more difficult when it came time for us to eat. I had laid the table in the dining-room as this was where Mary always served us, and without Kira there it was hard to keep the conversation going. I was still feeling bruised and ill-used, and try as I might it was not easy to remain civil.

'What's the matter?' Wren asked at a particularly tricky moment.

'Nothing at all,' I assured him.

'There's something,' he insisted. 'You're not acting normally.'

'And you know what my normal is? Honestly, you're imagining things.'

He lifted his head to stare me out, but I rose and said I needed to get the rice pudding out of the oven. When I returned, he tried again.

'Doug was here today, cutting down the old apple tree, wasn't he?'

'Yes.' I spooned two large serving spoons of the pudding into a bowl.

'And?'

'And nothing, we barely had time to say hello.'

'Oh, so that's why you're like a bear with a sore head.'

'What? Oh, don't be ridiculous — I'm just tired, it has nothing to do with Doug.'

He did not seem convinced. 'Well, I'm glad. I'd hate to think you'd fallen out after such a touching display when he dropped you home after the dance.'

'Were you spying on me?' I felt my hackles rise.

'No need to — you were very open about it.'

I remembered the kiss and how detached I had been from Doug's love-making. I almost told Wren that he had the wrong end of the stick — that I wasn't in a relationship with Doug, or anyone else for that matter, but then I realised it was safer if he thought I was.

My body seemed to have a mind of its own and as long as I was unable to control my reaction to Wren, it was just as well if he believed I was going out with someone else. It was infuriating, this hold he had over me, but I knew the attraction was based purely on hormones and had none of the finer feelings so necessary for sound, long-standing relationships.

What was it Lady Caroline Lamb had said about Byron? That he was mad, bad and dangerous to know! Well, I didn't think Wren was mad, nor really that he was bad, just not totally trustworthy. But for me at least, he was most definitely dangerous to know.

4

After that uncomfortable meal I tried to avoid being alone with Wren. I thought it rather rude of him to bring up Doug in that fashion anyway. What I did or didn't do with another man was none of his business after all. I wondered why he thought he had the right to criticise, because it had certainly felt as if he was criticising my behaviour.

Another blow came from Mary.

'Dr Carlton has decided Race no longer needs a personal trainer,' she said only days after Wren must have told her about my plan. 'As long as we keep walking him along the corridor twice a day he thinks he should be fine, and it doesn't take a professional to do that.'

My heart sank.

So now, not only was I sharing the house with two people I didn't wholly trust, but also the one outsider whose weekly visits had cheered up my day had been banned. I was beginning to feel totally cut off from the real world.

I thanked heaven that I still had Jean to offload to in my letters, otherwise if I'd had anywhere else to go, I think I might have resigned my post on the spot. I liked looking after Race, but the malignant atmosphere in the house was wearing me down.

I don't know whether to stay or look for something else, I admitted in a letter to Jean soon after the barn dance. *It's very unnerving here at the moment. Making conversation with Wren or Kira is a trial — I'm always nervous they'll run with tales about me to Mary even though I follow her instructions pretty much to the letter these days.*

Of course, I still try to stimulate Race because I believe it's good for him, but it's such a shame he has no outside visitors. It's true he never showed any particular reaction when Jane came, but she definitely kept him active and advised me on the best ways to ensure he retained some mobility.

I miss talking to Jane, too. It was reassuring for me to have someone to discuss my thoughts with and to be told my wish to improve Race's life was not all pie in the sky. Now I have no one to bounce ideas off of and that makes me doubt myself, I wrote to Jean.

Am I presuming too much — taking things the clinicians told me about Mum and Dad out of context then trying to apply them to Race? Perhaps his condition is degenerative and there's no chance of him making even the smallest recovery. I try to keep positive but I'm finding it quite difficult.

The one person keeping me sane is Doug — you remember the tree surgeon I told you about who took me to the barn dance? He's been quite attentive since, which is flattering, though I hope he isn't getting the wrong end of the stick as I'm not really looking for a love affair. He's good company and it's a relief to have someone I can be absolutely honest about things like my uneasiness around Wren and Kira and my belief that Race would be better served by a different doctor, and know my words will go no further. I can't see him that often, given my shifts, but we talk on the phone quite a bit which is a great release for me.

Mary mentioned I have some leave due, and I wondered if I could come and stay with you, Jean? I can't afford to book a holiday, and you were kind enough to say you'd have me at any time. Would it be convenient if I came over on the late May bank holiday, do you think?

★   ★   ★

Dear Jean was as good as her word, and as soon as she received my letter she called me to make the final arrangements.

I travelled up to Norfolk by train, taking little luggage as I didn't want to drag a heavy case across London to Liverpool Street Station.

My spirits began to rise the moment I left Great Haddows, and I remembered that awful feeling of dread I had experienced when I first arrived there. Then I'd had no reason to suppose my trepidation was anything more than fear of the unknown, but having lived there for two months I had to admit there was a negative atmosphere about the place.

Once the train had passed the built-up areas around Essex and moved on towards the flat open reaches of my home county, I started to really relax. The crushing weight of living in a stranger's house and having to curtail my own beliefs to accommodate those of my employer eased as I viewed the familiar countryside. Huge fields bordered with scrubby hedgerows — where they had been allowed to survive — and clear, wide-open skies. We flew past the landmarks I knew so well, each one of which announced I'd soon be home!

As I realised what I had just thought, sadness overwhelmed me. Of course, this was no longer my home — indeed, I had nowhere to call my own.

The memories the journey was evoking were just that — memories of a past when I was still protected by the love and support of my parents. Now I had to make my own way in the world and while I was determined to do so, I realised that the unhealthy atmosphere at Great Haddows and the thought that I would have to return there was colouring my outlook.

I caught a taxi from the station to the village where I had grown up, and as it turned into our old road a lump rose in my throat.

This was where I had learned so much and had such fun. In spite of wanting to wrap me in cotton wool at times, my parents had allowed me the luxury of making my own mistakes, the security of a loving home giving me the self-confidence to try new experiences.

That was why I had been able to manage after their deaths. Selling up and finding a position had not been easy, but I hadn't doubted I could do it; not to do so would have been to let them and their belief in me down.

The cab pulled up outside Briar Cottage and in all the kerfuffle of grabbing my bag and paying the fare I didn't have time to look across the road at our old home, which was all to the good.

People say you should never go back to somewhere you have been happy because the inevitable changes that will have taken place since will ruin your fond memories, but I was prepared for that.

I was determined that nothing would erase or lessen the place deep within me where I could relive those golden moments that had made living at Springfield such a golden time.

I knew the new owners would have made alterations — everyone had their own picture of an ideal home — and I was determined that I wouldn't allow them to upset me. The house in Farm Drive was no longer mine — but my home was safely stored in my heart.

'Jennie, my dear!' Jean was at the door, leaning on her stick.

We embraced and I had that wonderful feeling of acceptance, of love and goodwill and benevolence. How I had missed it!

'It's so good to see you . . . '

My voice faltered and I was afraid I'd cry.

'Come on into the kitchen. I've got the kettle on and I made your favourite rock cakes.'

I had to laugh. I had spent many happy hours baking with Jean when I was younger and had always insisted we make what I had called 'old-fashioned cakes.'

With my mother I had made cupcakes and chocolate brownies; with Jean I made the more traditional jam tarts and rock cakes. No matter that the jam regularly spilled over and burned, nor that the rock cakes came out of the oven as hard as bullets!

I loved imagining I was a 1950s

housewife in a frilly apron and full skirt. I had fallen in love with the era following a trip to Gressenhall Museum where a room kitted out in that rock'n'roll age had really caught my imagination, and thereafter I hankered after all things retro.

Luckily, Jean's own rock cakes, while firm enough to hold their shape, were rich and moist inside, and I settled down at her kitchen table to enjoy a trip down memory lane.

'The new people, Annie and Ross Wescott, are very nice,' Jean said, obviously deciding it was best to get the changes in the street over with as soon as possible. I knew she was right — I needed to lay those ghosts to rest. 'They help me out when they can, and I babysit their little boys.'

I was surprised and slightly shamed by the flash of envy that I felt — Jean was my honorary grandmother — but it went as quickly as it had come. Of course, time moved on, and it was wonderful she had another supportive family. It was only the help of neighbours that enabled her to remain independent. I was very pleased for her and also very grateful that I had my precious memories of our time together that no one could take away from me.

What had my mother said to me if I ever gave in to a childish display of jealousy? Something about having an abundance mentality and acknowledging there was enough love to go around. And she had been right — she had taught me that good times and love never die, and that had made her passing a little easier to bear.

'Annie is a physiotherapist and has been so helpful with all my aches and pains. As you know, there's a limit to how much therapy one can have on the NHS, so it's been wonderful having her across the road giving me free advice!'

My ears pricked up at this news. A physiotherapist? I wondered if I had the nerve to ask her about Race.

'The Wescotts are so excited at finally having enough room for their growing family,' Jean continued, 'And what they frequently say is that they can tell Springfield has always been a happy house as it had such a warm atmosphere.'

Her words pleased me. It was true, our house had always been a place of love and joy, and I realised I was glad the new family felt a positive ambience — it validated the many happy years we had shared there before them.

It was a family home and I knew it was right that another young family was making it their own. I found that once I had got used to the idea, I was actually glad Jean had developed a good relationship with her new neighbours. She deserved nothing less.

'Let's go into the sitting-room.'

She stood up and I could see it was less of a struggle for her than when I last saw her. Therapy had certainly improved her mobility.

I knew why Jean had ushered me into the kitchen rather than her lounge when I had first arrived: it had been to prepare me for the inevitable changes at Springfield before I actually saw them for myself.

Once I was sitting on her sofa I was able to stare directly at my old family home, and having been gently warned that the Westcotts had added a porch and installed new double-glazed windows, I found I could view them with equanimity and even admit they did improve the appearance of the house. I could see it hadn't been change for change's sake, but a sensible decision to make the place more comfortable.

Mum and Dad had been perfectly happy with the way things were because they had made the changes they wanted when they had moved in, and now it was someone else's turn.

'How are you finding your new job?' Jean asked once I'd relaxed back into our old familiar conversations. 'Have you made many friends?'

Had I? It didn't seem as if I had.

'Great Haddows is very isolated,' I explained. 'So there aren't any near neighbours. I really only see Mary, Wren and Kira regularly.'

'Doesn't your Mr Race have any visitors?'

'No, Mary says the doctor doesn't think it would be good for him.'

'Mary's the housekeeper?'

'Yes, and very correct but quite controlling. She's not very warm towards Race. I used to think it meant she didn't care about him, but it seems it's her way of coping with the fact that he may die — she doesn't want to get too close.' I pulled a face. 'I don't agree with that attitude. I think people should live right up until they die, but she's supported by the doctor.'

Jean raised her eyebrows. 'It does seem rather over-protective. When I'm laid up I love it when people come round. What do the nephew and niece say about it?'

'Not a lot. Wren works in London all week, so he's not around that much. I did try to talk to him about it, but he supported the status quo.'

'And his sister?'

'She's not the friendliest person I've ever met.' I sighed. 'I don't think she appreciates my being there and in fact I find her rather snide.'

'That's a shame — two young girls together, not getting on. I'd have thought your shared recent experience of losing your parents might have encouraged a bond between you.'

'Well, it hasn't. Kira works part-time at the local library, and when she's not there she spends hours reading books and mounds of papers on goodness knows what. She rarely talks to me.'

Jean always looked for the good in people. Now she said, 'I wonder if withdrawing from others is her way of coping with her parents' death? Losing your mother and father so young isn't easy.'

'I know.' I didn't mean to sound hard, but Jean's reaction showed me I had. She gave me one of her warm, all-embracing smiles.

'Oh, darling, I know you know, but

you did have warning it was coming so you could at least prepare for the awful day, no matter how hard it still was. Kira didn't, and it doesn't sound like she's come to terms with it yet. To lose both her mother and her father suddenly and brutally like that must have been a terrible shock.'

She was right, of course. I'd had time to adjust to the idea of my parents' death and had even done some of my mourning while they were still alive. I had known the prognosis for each of them, I was able to plan, and when the inevitable happened it had been expected.

'It may be she had unfinished business with them, and then learned she would never be able to clear the matter up. And an accident like that, which you said the coroner thought could have been avoided if her father hadn't been going so fast, must seem so arbitrary and unnecessary. I suspect everything is still very raw for her.'

'Yes, I can see that.'

I realised what Jean was suggesting

was very likely. Kira was only twenty-one — two years younger than I was — and she always seemed annoyed about something or someone! It could well be that she was looking for someone to blame. Perhaps that was why she was so angry about Race's situation. Here was her frail uncle, still alive however infirm, while his younger, healthier brother had died after answering his call for help.

'She probably feels the need to vent her anger and distress on someone, and as there are so few people around, she's focusing her attention on you. She's in a foreign land and even though she's with her brother, she must be lonely. Perhaps talking to her about your experience, about how it gets easier over time, might help?'

Dear Jean, she had a way of encouraging you to believe things would turn out well.

'I'll give it a try when I'm back at Great Haddows,' I promised, 'and I'll let you know whether it works.'

My week off did not seem very long at all and the days flashed by.

I enjoyed going out and about around all my old haunts and was pleased to find that my bereavement had not made me love them any the less. Many of my memories included days shared with my parents, but that didn't detract from the happiness I'd experienced both with them and now, as I returned alone.

I was learning that good times do not disappear but live on in the memory forever, full of laughter and joy.

'I've invited Annie and Ross over for a drink tonight,' Jean said on the day before I was due to return to Great Haddows. 'Stephanie Send from the end of the road has agreed to look after the little boys.'

'Little Stephanie from Glebe House who I used to look after?'

'Well, she's not so little any more. She's doing her A-levels this summer.'

How time had flown!

I realised I had hardly noticed much that had happened in the years I had cared for Mum and Dad. It had been my privilege to do so, but I knew I needed to get back out into circulation and live my own life.

The job at Great Haddows would tide me over, but I was looking forward to the time when I could make more permanent arrangements.

Jean was of the 'cocktail party' era, and whereas socialising had moved on, she hadn't. So she'd made delicious cheese straws and served little savoury biscuits with blobs of paté or soft cheese, and Annie Wescott later shared with me that the first time they had visited she and her husband had already eaten, and it had taken superhuman efforts on their part to force down the nibbles so lovingly provided.

'Now we know,' she whispered as Jean chatted with Ross, 'and only have something very light before popping over. Jean is such a dear and we wouldn't want to hurt her feelings. We're so lucky to have her as a neighbour.'

'She tells me how lucky she is to have you. I understand you've been giving her physiotherapy?'

Annie nodded. 'Well, sort of. I've just been showing her the best way to manage her arthritis, and it does seem to have helped her.'

'My client in Kent could do with someone like you.' Much as I felt like trapping her in a corner and telling her all Race's symptoms, I knew I couldn't, but I did wonder if she might be able to give me a few pointers.

'Tell me,' was all she said.

Having been given permission I explained how Race was so slow on his feet and so disinterested in everything, how he did seem to be improving with more intensive input from Jane and myself. But now that had stopped, and I blamed myself as I had planned to go against the doctor's wishes. I finished by telling her that I was left wondering what to do for the best.

'Hmm, odd that the doctor hasn't referred your client to a physio.' She put her head on one side as she considered what I had told her. 'It's quite usual for medics to involve physical therapists in such cases.'

'This doctor doesn't seem to think it a good idea, perhaps because Race is always so dozy.'

'Well, that's another thing — from what you describe it almost seems as if Race is 'spaced out' somehow — you know, as a result of being given too high a dose of antipsychotic drugs. What medication is he on?'

I was embarrassed to admit, 'I don't know. The housekeeper deals with all that — I just give him what's in the dosette box she prepares.'

Annie frowned. 'But surely there's a drug chart you have to sign to confirm what you've given and when? That must say what the tablets are and what the dosage is.'

I shook my head. 'No. When I asked about that the housekeeper said that as my client lives in his own home we didn't need to do that.'

'Oh, that is really poor practice.' Annie sucked air between her teeth. 'And it leaves you wide open if anything goes wrong. I'm sure everything his doctor prescribes is completely as it should be, but you must have heard the expression 'chemical cosh'? It's when a patient is over-prescribed narcotics leaving him rather like a zombie, quiet and slow in movement. Drugs do interact, and if the doctor only visits irregularly he might not pick it up. It's really up to carers like you to point it out.'

I pulled a face. I didn't see Mary or Dr Carlton being willing to listen to me, especially not about something like this.

'You really need to look into it,' Annie insisted. 'I'm happy to show you some general exercises you could do with someone like him to improve his mobility, but if your client is too heavily prescribed there's an increased risk of falling, so it really needs to be sorted out.'

I didn't sleep well that night. Annie's

words had reignited my concerns about Race, and I knew I had to do something. But what?

I was sure Mary would dismiss any fears I might raise, and going on past experience, Dr Carlton would not be open to discussion. Yet I owed it to Race to ensure he was safe, and from what Annie had said, only a drug review would tell us if he was receiving the correct type and dose of medication.

Who could I turn to?

Before he had blabbed to Mary about my intention to take Race outside I might have tried Wren, but now I knew I couldn't trust him. And Kira, with her sharp words and belief that her uncle's life wasn't worth living, was hardly better.

Then I thought of Doug, solid and dependable, and I heaved a sigh of relief. There was no romantic spark between us — or at least, there wasn't on my part — and that made conversations easier. He was someone I could speak to in confidence, and who would give me sensible advice.

When I finally slept I dreamed I was walking Race outside at Great Haddows. Rather than shuffling, he was picking up his feet and striding out.

Nearby, next to the drain by the back door, Doug was pouring away a liquid from an old-fashioned bottle which had the picture of a skull and crossbones with *Poison* written on its side.

When I woke I thought how odd it was what the subconscious came up with when the mind was troubled, but it seemed to have done the trick as I felt more relaxed and actually allowed myself to believe that soon everything would be sorted.

I couldn't possibly have known what terrors lay ahead . . .

5

It was a perfect day as the train sped me back through the Kent countryside, the blue skies and bright sunlight enhancing the early summer scenery. White apple blossom touched with pink bobbed gently in the breeze, and the candles were forming on the horse chestnuts. There was still a scattering of late tulips, and the dog roses and wild honeysuckle were coming into their own.

As it was a Sunday, which meant 'unsocial hours', I was geared up to be very firm with John Hancock and agree a price before I got into his taxi. Weekend rates or not, I was determined not to be ripped off. I didn't intend to get caught out as I had on my expensive late-night arrival at Great Haddows when he had overcharged me.

As it turned out, I didn't need to. I

had let Mary know which train I was catching and she had sent out the cavalry.

'Jennie, over here!' a familiar voice called.

I was startled to see Wren waiting for me. Startled and yet — heaven help me! — in some strange way, so very pleased. My heart began to race as he walked towards me and my mouth became so dry I found it hard to answer.

He didn't seem to notice.

'Mary asked me to come and collect you,' he explained.

So he hadn't come of his own accord because he wanted to help me. How ridiculous to feel disappointed at that knowledge, but I did.

'Did you have a good break?'

I nodded, still tongue-tied.

As he drove through the valley he hummed to himself, apparently unaware of the oppressive silence. Part of me would have loved to talk to him — to tell him about what Annie had said and enlist his help — but I knew if I did I

123

risked things getting back to Mary before I had worked out a plan of action.

I wondered why he couldn't see how controlling Mary was regarding Race's life, but had to admit neither he nor his sister gave the impression of being very interested. And that surprised me because, although I found Kira hard work, I still clung to the hope that, deep down, Wren was a caring individual.

I gasped as we turned into the long drive and I saw that the acid pinks and yellows of the early azaleas had been superseded by the vibrant blooms of the towering rhododendrons. What a lot could happen in a week, I thought, as I luxuriated in their heavenly scent.

'Everywhere looks so beautiful!' I couldn't stop myself exclaiming. 'It's such a shame Race can't enjoy the grounds.'

Wren eyed me, an amused smile on his lips. 'Still wanting to help him break out?' he asked. 'I don't think Mary would be happy to hear you.'

His response told me in no uncertain

terms that he retained his belief that the housekeeper knew best, which was presumably why he had told her of my plan in the first place. I bit my lip. I mustn't say a word until I had decided the best way to tackle the situation.

The delicate flowers of the sweet-smelling wisteria ramped across the red brick frontage of the house, and as I looked up to admire the dripping purple blooms I caught sight of Kira's face at Race's bedroom window. I must have shown my surprise, because Wren laughed.

'Mary hasn't been feeling too well while you've been away,' he explained, 'so Kira has been watching Race from nine at night 'til after his breakfast next morning. She's no Florence Nightingale, but even she can tuck him up in bed and deal with his medication! It's given Mary a bit of a break.'

When we went into the kitchen, Mary didn't look as if she'd had much of a break. She was sitting at the table, clutching her stomach.

'Are you OK?' I asked, even though it was patently clear she wasn't.

'I don't feel so good. Hope I'm not getting the bug that's going round. I really thought I'd be over it by now.'

In spite of the warmth of the day, she pulled her cardigan more tightly around herself. She didn't look well at all.

'Why don't you go home to bed? I can manage here and if you are sickening for something, you don't want to give it to Mr Race.'

When I spoke with her I always used Race's title, aware she would think it too familiar not to.

At first she seemed unsure how to take my offer, giving me a suspicious look.

'Kira and I can manage between us,' I urged. 'I understand she's already been doing the nights.'

Wren smiled at her encouragingly, which seemed to do the trick. She gave him — not me — a grateful nod. 'Well, if you're sure it's no trouble.'

It wasn't, not really.

Kira was only too pleased to be relieved. I thought about the conversation I'd had with Jean and wondered how I should go about trying to establish some kind of rapport with her. But she didn't seem keen to stay in my company and gathered up the file she'd been reading while sitting with Race, doubtless off to the library.

I found her fascination with it inexplicable. The room faced north and was quite dark; the only window it once had looked out across the garden and must have let in some light, but had been lost when it became the door to Race's study.

Mary told me he'd had the room added on to the house to give him and Susan a modern office from which to run their businesses. I had seen inside the office once when Mary was vacuuming in there. The view from its large window was bright and colourful across the garden — much nicer than the library, even given the fact that in here there were rows of box files rather than leather-bound books.

I had once asked Kira why she didn't sit in there instead, and she replied she had tried it when she'd first come to Great Haddows, but preferred to sit where her father might have done as a child.

'Hello, Race.' I gave him my usual greeting. 'How are you feeling today?'

'OK.'

The words were so softly spoken I could hardly believe I had heard them!

As ever he was sitting in his chair, but his posture was different — he wasn't as slumped as usual — and I bent forward to look directly into his face. His eyes, usually so dead and disinterested, were brighter and they held my gaze.

What miracle had happened here?

'What have you been doing while I was away?'

But that was too much. Race might have been more alert, but the base line he started from had been very low, and whereas his eyes followed me across the room and he even smiled back at me, he was in no state to enter into a conversation.

Nevertheless, I was extremely excited and wondered what could have happened for him to improve so dramatically.

I soon found out.

I helped him to the bathroom to clean his teeth after his supper and was pleased to see he was much steadier than before.

I then went to tidy up round his chair. A tissue was stuck down the side of the seat cushion, and I slipped my hand in to remove it, only to find something small and hard beside it. I grasped it with my finger and thumb and pulled it out.

It was a pill.

Not a pristine pill but one that had been in someone's mouth; the sharp edges had dissolved leaving a ragged outline. There was no doubt it was one of Race's tablets. I put my hand back down the gap between the chair arm and the seat and after some careful exploration withdrew a further thirteen of them.

I knew from the colour and shape which ones they were, even if I didn't know what they did. He took them at night and early in the morning when he woke up.

This meant it was the night carer — me, or when I was off duty, Mary — who gave them to him, and we both knew that it was necessary to watch Race once they were in his mouth to ensure he didn't spit them back out.

Kira didn't. Mary must have been very unwell not only to forget to tell her, but also to overlook the debris down the side of the chair; normally she checked everywhere and everything.

I looked up and saw that Race was returning from his ablutions without prompting.

I helped him settle in bed and began tidying around him. I picked up an old leather-bound book from the chest of drawers next to him, pretty sure it must have been what Kira had been reading when she sat with him until he dozed off.

Seeing it my hand, Race became quite agitated.

'The border's the key!' he cried, waving his arms at me. 'Green three, blue beside, bush above ... green three, blue beside, bush above!'

Even allowing for his slight slurring, I couldn't make sense of his words.

Although I was pleased he was using his voice, I didn't want him to become distressed, so I slipped the book under the box of tissues on the windowsill and handed him a copy of a magazine I guessed Mary had been reading before she went off sick. He took it, and after a quick glance, pushed it aside, but it did the trick and he didn't seem to remember the book.

However, I was now left with a dilemma.

Should I reinstate Race's tablets — give them to him now as usual? Or should I omit them in light of the fact that he appeared to be doing so much better without them?

I wasn't a doctor and it wasn't my

place to decide long-term, but I did wonder if it wouldn't be a good thing for Dr Carlton to see how much perkier Race was without the drugs before I gave them to him again.

Then it struck me — the person who could best advise me was surely a dispensing pharmacist who would know how various drugs interacted.

I remembered Mary telling me the nearest chemist was in Pashton, just five miles away, and I thought it likely that was where she picked up Race's prescription. That helped me make my decision. I'd give Race all his other drugs but hold off on the tablets he'd spat out until I had spoken to the pharmacist there.

The next day I approached Kira. I wanted to ask her to watch Race while I popped out, and thought it would be a good opportunity to try and have a chat with her.

She was on a late shift at the library and said she would be happy to take the papers she was reading and sit with him.

'Were you a librarian in South Africa?' I asked.

'No.' She didn't encourage confidences.

'It's just you seem to like books so much, especially those about Haddows.' I picked up a dusty tome from the top of the pile next to her. '*The Design of Sixteenth Century Houses*,' I read aloud. 'Are you interested in architecture?'

She paused for a moment before replying, 'Yes, I want to study it at uni.'

'That's really interesting,' I said, grasping at straws. 'I want to study horticulture and landscape design, and I love reading about historical gardens. Maybe we could have a chat about them sometime?'

'We're both so busy . . . '

She let her response hang in the air without actually refusing, but strengthened by Jean's words about how lonely the girl might be underneath it all, I didn't give up and grasped the bull by the horns.

'When my parents died I got into a bit of a rut.' I lowered my voice and gave her what I hoped was a sympathetic smile. 'I rarely went out and buried myself in my gardening books. I was lucky because our family had a dear older friend who came to my rescue and insisted I got on with the business of living.'

I paused before continuing, 'It must be very hard for you having no one around who knew your parents, apart from your brother. I found talking about my parents to people who'd also loved them very consoling.'

She looked up at me then, and I could see tears were not far away.

'I miss them so much!' It came out in a rush. 'Wren and I do share memories, but he's been more able to move forward. I suppose it's because he's still working for the same company in pretty much the same job, albeit in a different country. Things haven't changed that much for him. He's in contact with people back home and he's made new friends in London and they're helping him . . . '

She broke off, as if she'd said too much.

'Had you thought of maybe joining a club or taking up a hobby that would mean you'd meet new people?'

She gave me what my father would have called an old-fashioned look.

'You're a fine one to talk! You haven't, and you don't know anyone here, either.'

I had thought I'd been making head-way, but the shutters had come down again.

'No, that's true. Perhaps it was a silly idea,' I back-tracked. 'But I did find it helpful to have someone to share things with and I thought you might, too. Anyway, I just wanted you to know that if you ever want to talk — not just about your parents, but about anything — I'm here. If I'm truthful, I'd rather welcome it . . . as you rightly said, I'm a new girl here, too, and haven't made any friends yet.'

My words seemed to annoy her.

135

'Really?' she said. 'And there I thought you had.'

I sensed her withdrawal and knew there would be no point in continuing the conversation.

I thought what a prickly person she could be and wondered what I had said to upset her suddenly.

Still, I'd made a start, and I hoped that things might progress further during a later exchange.

For a moment she had let her disinterested air drop and showed me the vulnerable girl beneath — it was a girl I recognised from my own bereavement and one I wanted to help.

★ ★ ★

There were no customers in the chemist's shop when I arrived, which made it easier to talk to the pharmacist on duty. I didn't want to give too much away, knowing how Mary hated the locals getting information about Race, but even though we'd never met, I was quite sure he knew who I was — there are no secrets in country villages — so it was difficult to be circumspect.

I explained that 'my client' had been spitting out his pills and while that had been worrying to discover, it did appear that not taking them had lessened his general fatigue and lethargy.

The chemist nodded wisely. 'It's very sad, I remember Mr Engleton was a fine figure of a man. I grew up in Haddows and often saw him.'

As I had feared, the chemist had recognised who I was talking about at once!

'What medications is he on?' he asked.

'I was hoping you could tell me,' I replied. 'The housekeeper deals with the record-keeping, but I'm assuming she gets his prescription here.'

'I'm afraid you're wrong. The Engletons did bring their scripts to me, but since Mrs Engleton died her husband must have gone elsewhere.' He thought for a moment. 'Which doctor does he see?'

'He doesn't use the local GP practice. He has a private chap come down from London.'

'That would probably account for it. I expect he arranges for the medications to be sent to the house. You say the housekeeper deals with it all?' he asked. 'Why don't you ask her, then?'

It was a reasonable question — why didn't I? I struggled to think how to respond. I could hardly say she seemed to prefer Race to be quiet and compliant, though now I thought about it, I realised she did. I shrugged.

'Difference of opinion, eh?'

He could clearly add two and two.

'Well, if she doesn't want to tell you, I'd speak to the doctor. Some drugs have multiple uses. For example, certain epilepsy drugs can also be used as anti-depressants. If a person is on multiple medications they can have what is called 'a high anticholinergic burden' which can lead to a number of side effects, including fatigue.'

'Should inform the doctor?'

He nodded. 'Yes, you should.'

It was all very well to be told that, but quite another to work out how to do so. I didn't have Dr Carlton's details so couldn't contact him directly, but I was worried that if I went to Mary not only would she be angry I'd spoken to the pharmacist, but also livid that I hadn't reinstated Race's drugs. I was sure she would do so at once so that by the time the doctor arrived, Race would have reverted to his previous inertia, and nothing would be done.

★   ★   ★

As I pulled up in front of Great Haddows I saw Doug coming out of the gardener's cottage and waved. 'What are you doing here?' I asked him.

'Just came to sort out payment for the work I carried out.' He looked surprised to see me. 'Kira said you had gone out when I called at the house for you.'

'Only on a quick errand. Did you

want something?'

'Just wanted to know how you were now Jane no longer visits.'

'I didn't know you knew Jane?'

'Umm, I don't, not really, but I know of her. Brian told me Mary got rid of her because she thought it a good idea for you to take Mr Race outside. I suppose she told Mary about the plan.'

'I know who told Mary, and it wasn't Jane.' Just the thought of it made me steam. 'It was Wren — it had to be! I asked him to help me get Race downstairs and he refused. Next thing I know Mary sends Jane packing — it doesn't take a genius to work out.'

'No, I suppose not.' Doug had appeared rather tense during our exchange, but now he relaxed. 'I wanted to ask if you'd like to come out for a drink one evening?'

It would make nice change, I thought, but my duties wouldn't allow it while Mary was off.

'I can't while Mary's sick, but if you've a moment, we can have a coffee in the kitchen?'

'I'd like that.'

I led the way into the house and filled the automatic coffee maker. Truth to tell I was relieved to have someone I trusted to talk to. I still couldn't decide what to do and it would be helpful to sound out ideas with Doug.

'I'm in a bit of a quandary,' I said and proceeded to tell him all that had happened, finding the tablets, the fact that Race seemed so much better, and what the pharmacist had said.

'The problem is,' I finished off, 'I don't know how to broach the subject. I think Mary will be too cross to listen, but if Race needs a medication review, I have to tell someone.'

'You do.' Doug nodded, nursing his coffee in his big, capable hands. 'And the best person to go to is Mary. I know you find her a bit officious, but we've agreed, haven't we, that the reason she protects Mr Race so carefully is because she cares and can't bear to think of anything happening to him? But if his tablets really are the cause of his problems she'll be keen to get the doctor down to see him. Brian told me she'll be back tomorrow, so you can speak to her then.'

It made sense.

'I will and thank you for your help.'

He had finished his coffee and stood to leave.

'My pleasure.'

He caught my hand and held it for a moment.

'Remember, you can come to me any time. I don't like the thought of you here, with Wren.'

'I'm OK.'

The sound of Wren's name reminded me of how I'd reacted when he had taken my arm at the barn dance. Why couldn't I feel about Doug the way I felt about Wren? Doug was straight and caring and kind, while all I could say about Wren was that he seemed to sit on the fence. I knew I couldn't have trusted him with this conversation, yet it appeared I was still attracted to him.

After Doug had gone I checked on Race and then dealt with the laundry.

Kira joined me and I told her what Doug had said about Mary returning the next day.

'Oh, that's what he was doing here.' Kira gave me one of her knowing looks, all signs of the grieving daughter now firmly hidden. I got the impression she saw it as a weakness. 'I wondered why he was visiting Mary half an hour ago. I saw him at her front door.'

'Nearer an hour,' I said as I loaded the washing-machine. 'He went to query a bill with Brian and then came and had a coffee here.'

'Did he now?' Again, that questioning gaze as if she didn't believe me. 'I was sure it was only thirty minutes ago and it was Mary talking to him at the door. Anyway, he seems smitten with you.'

'Rubbish! He's just being helpful, that's all.' I didn't want to hear how she interpreted our relationship. I wondered why Kira was always so scratchy and what she could hope to gain by saying it was Mary and not Brian that Doug had been talking to. He would hardly have gone back to the cottage after our meeting.

'If you say so.'

She smiled sweetly, her expression indicating she didn't believe a word of it.

★ ★ ★

Despite what Doug had said to me, I wasn't looking forward to the showdown with Mary and I waited until Race was up and dressed before broaching the subject.

'Don't you think Race is much more alert than he was?' I asked and awaited the denial.

'Yes, now that you mention it, I do. He's even been saying a few nonsense sentences. Have you heard anything?'

'No, not really. As you say, it was only nonsense.' I was amazed she agreed with me.

'I wonder why it is.' She shrugged her shoulders and shook her head.

That was my chance.

I took a deep breath and told her about the missed tablets. I stressed it wasn't Kira's fault, saying if I hadn't been warned at the hospice about patients sometimes hiding their tablets in their mouth and then spitting the out when the care-giver had gone, I would never have considered such a possibility. I then told her what the pharmacist had said.

'I didn't want to bother you while you were ill, which is why I went to the chemist.'

A white lie, but I could hardly tell her the reason I hadn't reported it to her was because I thought she would override any concerns and simply reintroduce the tablets.

'The pharmacist suggested Race should have a medication review.'

'It sounds an excellent idea.' She even smiled at me! 'I'll contact Dr Carlton and let him know what's happened — and

Mr Landon as well. We all want the best for Mr Race. Well done you for noticing it.'

To say I was flabbergasted would have been an understatement!

So Doug had been right — when it came to care, Mary *was* concerned for Race.

I felt rather guilty that I had doubted her, but knowing how severe she could be, I didn't entirely trust her not to have a go at Kira, so that night I made another attempt to build, if not a friendship, then at least an understanding . . .

I'd wondered if Kira had noticed any difference in Race when she'd been standing in for Mary and decided to start the conversation by asking her. As ever, she was in the library, poring over old history books. She thought for a moment before answering.

'He did seem a bit brighter by the end of the week, but I put that down to not having to put up with Mary all day! She can be very rigid. Trouble is, I didn't have much to do with Race before that — you know nursing isn't my thing — so I couldn't really say to what degree he improved or deteriorated.'

I hadn't expected much more — I felt Kira was too wound up by the link between her uncle and her parents' death to have paid much attention to Race. I could tell it was not that she lacked compassion, rather that her own grief so overwhelmed her she didn't have the space for anything else.

'Actually, something amazing happened while you were looking after him.' I decided to make it sound as if her oversight had been a positive thing, which in a way, it had been. I didn't want her to think I was criticising her. 'Race has a habit of spitting out his tablets, and we forgot to tell you that. When I came back I found them down the side of his chair. But I also noticed how much more alert he was.'

Her eyes narrowed as she listened, waiting, no doubt, to see if I blamed her for not properly fulfilling her duties. I hurried on.

'It was easier for me as I'd been away for a whole week and so I saw a big change, whereas people in the house were seeing Race every day and would have missed his gradual improvement.'

Kira relaxed somewhat at my words.

'I suppose he did seem more interested towards the end of the week — catching my eye instead of just staring straight ahead.'

'Yes, that's what I noticed,' I said. 'And he was . . . well, you couldn't call it speaking, exactly, because it didn't make any sense, but he did speak, which I hadn't heard him do before.'

'Yes, he did,' agreed Kira. 'But I didn't really register what he was saying.' She looked down at her feet. 'I suppose you think me uncaring?'

'Not at all. We're not all cut out to be carers.'

She gave a big sigh.

'Well, I know I'm not, anyway. It might have been different if we'd known Race when we were young, but Dad made a complete break with him after they argued, so we didn't. Dad met and married Mum in South Africa, so we had aunts and uncles there, but we'd only heard vaguely of 'Uncle Race'.'

'That's rather sad.'

'I'm not sure . . . there was something odd about my Dad's relationship with his brother. He didn't like even to mention his name and was determined we should have nothing to do with him. That's why it was such a shock when he arranged for him and Mum to come to England the minute he received Race's letter. It was so out of character.'

I knew I had to be very careful how I responded. Kira was opening up to me, but I had experience of how quickly she could turn and shut down any conversation if the wrong thing was said.

'Do you think it was their ages?' I asked gingerly. 'I understand people do want to make amends as they get older in case fate intervenes and means they never can.' I didn't like to use the 'death' word in case it set her off.

'I don't really think so. I mean, if it was, I'd have expected him to have been talking about Race before he received the letter — saying he wanted to make up — because he was a very open man and we didn't have secrets in our family. But there was nothing like that. One day we were living our normal lives, the next the letter arrived and Dad was booking his and Mum's flights. There was no discussion and when we tried to talk to him, it was clear something was weighing heavily on his mind. But when we queried it he said we were imagining things and wouldn't tell us.'

'But you felt something was wrong?'

'Yes, both Wren and I were sure there was more to the trip than Dad was letting on. Then, when we heard they'd been killed in the car crash it was almost as if it confirmed our worst fears — that Dad was involved in something dangerous and wanted to protect us by telling us nothing.'

I was shocked. 'You mean you don't think the crash was an accident?'

She shrugged helplessly. 'We don't really know. I know it sounds far-fetched, but the more we looked into it, the more it seemed unlikely that someone with Dad's driving skills would have misjudged the road and driven so fast that they crashed. He was an experienced rally driver, after all. And Mum hated speed and was always telling him to slow down, so it just didn't ring true.'

'But if it wasn't an accident . . . ?'

I didn't want to hear the answer. I felt myself going cold. I gazed out over the garden, hoping the blousy abundance of summer would calm me.

Kira shook her head. 'Impossible to say. It's just a nagging feeling that something isn't quite right here.'

I turned to stare at Kira. The words she had used were so similar to my own silent mantra: something at Great Haddows wasn't quite right.

'Did you ever see the letter that Race sent to your father?'

'No, Dad took it with him. When we came over for the funeral we searched through his belongings to try and find it but he must have thrown it away.'

'You have no idea what it contained or why he felt it so urgent to dash over to England to see his brother?'

Again, she shook her head. 'No.'

I didn't know what to say.

My bereavement had been hard but I had known it was coming, which meant when it happened I had been able to cope. Now she had told me the circumstances of her parents' death I could see why Kira was so brittle. Not only had she been unprepared, but she was worried there might be more to it than the official line.

I wondered if it was simply her imagination, a need to give a senseless death meaning, but from what she said, Wren thought this, too, and he was no fool. And then there was that all-pervading atmosphere that we both felt, that all was not as it should be at Great Haddows.

'I'm so sorry,' I said.

It was as if a switch had been flicked and she morphed back into the casual, indifferent niece.

'Why should you be? It wasn't your fault.'

She started reading her book, indicating our conversation was over.

★   ★   ★

In spite of Mary's praise, I was still nervous of what might be the reaction of Dr Carlton. He was the clinician in charge, after all, and he might override us, so I was delighted when Mary informed me he had been and confirmed the medication needed to be changed. He'd visited on my day off so I didn't have to suffer his superior attitude, but I was pleased he had prescribed a different regime that I was informed would be better for Race.

Only it wasn't.

Within a few days of starting the new capsules, Race's fatigue increased and his interest waned. This time I was not too worried, I was sure Mary would have noticed, too, and would simply call Dr Carlton back, but I was mistaken.

'Oh, this is too much, Jennie!' she exclaimed when I raised the subject. 'Dr Carlton has only just changed the medication and you are finding fault already! You have to realise that Mr Race is a sick man and hoping a new wonder pill is going to work miracles is simply setting yourself up to be disappointed. Even when he was more alert he didn't make any sense, and the best we can hope for now is to keep him comfortable.'

I was stunned that Mary couldn't see the deterioration in Race, but recognised she was not going to change her mind.

In desperation I sought out Kira again.

'You know you said you noticed Race was a bit brighter and even said a few words when he was off his previous meds,' I reminded her. 'Well, I wondered how you found him now? I think the new drugs are just as bad as the others.'

She seemed strangely reluctant to engage in the conversation.

'I don't want to appear unhelpful, Jennie, but I really don't spend enough time with him to be able to say one way or the other. I don't want to get involved, and besides, I don't have any evidence to give a view.'

And that, as I told Doug, was the problem. Apart from me, no one spent enough time with Race to be aware of how he had changed.

Doug and I had taken to meeting up at the Black Swan pub in Pashton when I was off-duty. I was in two minds about doing so. On the one hand I didn't want him to read too much into our relationship — I saw him as a friend and nothing more — but on the other it was a relief to get away from Great Haddows sometimes and to be able to talk freely.

'I wouldn't rely on Wren or Kira for any help,' he said. 'They're pretty secretive, don't you think? Him spending most of his time in London and she reading every old book she can lay her hands on.'

Although she hadn't held me to any confidence, I didn't feel it right to share what Kira had told me regarding her fears about her parents' car crash, so kept quiet on that front. However, I was surprised he knew so much about them and I said so.

'Oh, Brian and I are in the same darts team,' he said. 'And he's a great talker.'

'I don't know that I'd call them secretive — more stand-offish, I'd say.'

Perhaps I was being disingenuous given what I had learned from Kira, but was suspecting your father was not responsible for the crash that caused their deaths and trying to prove it, actually secretive? Not really, I decided. Indeed, on reflection after speaking to

Kira I had thought it unlikely to be true. More probably she and Wren were trying to exonerate their father.

'Well, she was very odd at that dance — muscling into our set — she said she did it so she could partner me, but that wasn't why.'

I remembered that I had found it odd, too. Then I had a thought . . .

'She's always reading up about the Engletons and Great Haddows,' I said. 'I suppose she may be searching for some roots now their parents are dead.'

The more I thought about it, the more I liked the idea. Kira was having something of a crisis, unable to accept her parents' death with no relatives in England to turn to except her equally grieving brother. Perhaps she was comforted by the thought of previous generations of Engletons and their ordered lives at Great Haddows.

'Why would that interest her? More likely she's looking for something like buried treasure that she and her brother can claim as the last of the Engletons!'

I laughed. 'Is that likely? Is there some legend about it?'

'Nah, not really. Mind you, Mr Race is a very wealthy man so it could be they're looking for the treasure they seek by staking a claim to his house and possessions! He's incredibly rich,' he repeated, 'And with his wife dead, they *are* his next-of-kin.'

'But surely, he can leave whatever he likes to whomsoever he likes — Great Haddows isn't entailed, is it?'

'No, it isn't and yes, he can, and I expect he wrote a new will after his wife died. However, they may think that if they stay around long enough he'll make another one and maybe leave everything to them.'

It sounded a bit far-fetched to me. It wasn't as if Wren or Kira spent hours with Race trying to worm their way into his affections — and there was another reason.

'No, he couldn't. I'm sure any solicitor would say Race no longer has the capacity to do so.'

Doug considered this and then said, 'You're right — and maybe it's time someone pointed that out to them.'

*　*　*

I thought no more about our exchange until the following week when Wren sought me out in Race's room.

'Do you know anything about this?' he demanded, waving a letter in my face.

'I won't know until you show it to me, will I? And please don't raise your voice, it upsets Race.'

'It seems that you're just as keen to control him as the others!'

Wren was not making much sense.

'Could you please tell me what this is about?' I tried to remain calm in the face of his anger.

'Just what I'd like to know. Kira and I have received this letter from Mr Landon, telling us he's coming down for a meeting to advise us of the long-term arrangements for Race. He seems to imply that we're causing difficulties here and need to move on. Has that come from you?'

'Of course not! I don't know anything about it.'

He stood watching me for so long that it became uncomfortable, as if he was trying to read my face.

Then he turned to Race, who was dozing in his chair, but he said nothing.

'It's a shame you and Kira aren't more involved with him,' I said, which wasn't very diplomatic, but he was their uncle after all, and since I had been there Wren hadn't spent much time with him at all.

'We've had other things on our mind — things to help Race.' My words had obviously stung. 'Things aren't necessarily as they seem.'

'Obviously not.'

He seemed about to say something else, but thought better of it and left the room.

My knees were trembling so much that I sat down on Race's bed. Was it because I felt guilty? It was true that I knew nothing about the solicitor's impending visit, but recalling my conversation with Doug, I still felt mortified. Had he mentioned it to Brian, and had it got back to Mr Landon that way? We hadn't meant anything by it, but perhaps Brian and Mary had taken it seriously and contacted the solicitor.

I realised it wasn't just guilt that was making me feel low — it was also the thought that Wren might be leaving. Even though we hadn't seen much of each other since the dance, I found the news that he and Kira could be going quite depressing.

I told myself that I was being ridiculous, that there had never been anything between us, but my heart didn't want to listen. How could I be so upset that a man I barely knew, hardly ever saw and couldn't trust, would no longer be around?

An answer nudged at the edges of my mind but was so outlandish that I firmly dismissed it. According to Doug,

Wren Engleton was nothing more than a man on the make, so how could I possibly feel anything for him?

I got to my feet and went to clean Race's bathroom. I needed to do something mindless and repetitive if I were not to ruminate on the foolishness of my heart.

6

Mr Landon was a suave, handsome man of indeterminate years — his manicured hands and carefully dressed grey hair suggested his appearance meant a lot to him, and when he frowned I noticed his forehead only moved infinitesimally. In fact his whole face remained pretty static, which told its own tale. His beautifully cut suit spoke of expensive Italian tailoring, and when he checked the time, his watch was a Rolex.

There were six of us in the room apart from him: Kira and Wren, Mary and Brian, and Dr Carlton and myself. The atmosphere was tense and I wondered why I had been included in the summons. I soon found out.

'As you know, I am Mr Engleton's financial advisor,' the solicitor continued. 'I have been for years, and I think it fair to say that he and his late wife trusted me implicitly.'

He seemed to almost preen for a moment.

'When Susan died, Race was so upset that he asked me to take over everything, which is what I did, and this in fact proved a godsend when he became so ill. We've all been hoping Race will recover, but after all this time I think we have to accept that is not going to happen.'

He paused again, then turned to Dr Carlton.

'Doctor, would you update us on Race's condition and what you think the future holds?'

'Certainly.' Dr Carlton slipped into his most-important-man-in-the-room mode. 'As you know, I've been treating his symptoms conservatively, and hoped the medication would improve things, but in fact thanks to this young lady here —' he gave me a thin smile — 'we discovered they were actually making things worse. Consequently, I did a complete medical review and changed the drugs he was on, and thankfully he is now less anxious. However, he remains somewhat agitated, and we must do all we can to try and overcome this.'

My heart sank as he spoke. True to form he was going for the easy option: keeping Race on strong medication that meant he was no trouble. What was it Annie had called it? A chemical cosh.

'And have we any idea what is causing his agitation?' Mr Landon threw the question out to the room.

Mary put up her hand as if she were in school and the solicitor nodded at her to speak.

'Well, it's a bit embarrassing . . . I wouldn't want to upset anyone . . . '

'I'm sure no one will be offended, Mary, we simply want to get to the bottom of things so we can make Race's life as comfortable as possible for him.'

She gave an uneasy smile and ducked her head. I had never seen her look uncomfortable before, and as I was sitting next to her I was able to catch the almost artful glint that came into her eyes which others couldn't see.

'I have noticed that Mr Race gets very upset when his nephew and niece have spent time with him — especially his niece,' she said in a humble voice. She raised her eyes and faced the siblings. 'I'm so sorry to have to say this, but it's only what I have observed.'

'That's rubbish!' Wren looked like thunder and I could see an angry pulse throbbing on his neck.

'I wish it were,' Mary continued. 'But in fact even Jennie noticed it, didn't you, dear?'

She turned to look at me.

'No, I can't say that I did actually — ' I began, but she cut me off.

'You remember, when you came back from Norfolk, you were so concerned about him that you actually went to speak to the pharmacist at Pashton because I was unwell and you didn't want to worry me.'

'But that was because I thought Race's medication was wrong for him, not because I thought anyone was upsetting him.'

'Yes, but what you noticed was that Race was agitated and talking gibberish — you told me that,' she said triumphantly. 'And the only change to his normal routine was that Kira became involved in his care. That's right, isn't it?'

'Yes . . . No! I mean yes, Kira was caring for him at night, but no, I didn't think his anxiety was because of her.'

'You're a very kind-hearted girl and I know you don't want to think ill of anyone,' Dr Carlton broke in. 'But you must admit you wanted me to do a medical review because you were so worried about Race.'

'He needed a medication review, yes, but — '

Doctor Carlton and Mary were determined I shouldn't say more than they wanted heard.

'I feel that having Race's niece and nephew here is not conducive to his well-being, and that it would be best for all concerned if they left now.'

Dr Carlton attempted to give a

regretful smile, but to me it didn't quite come off.

For whatever reason he wanted them gone, and the accusations meant it was plain there was no way they could stay. If they argued against it they would appear to be callously indifferent to their uncle's welfare now that a medical man had put Race's deterioration squarely in their court.

'This is most unfortunate.' Mr Landon addressed the siblings. 'But you do see, don't you? We have to listen to the doctor, and if he thinks Race would be better off without your presence, you will need to go.'

'Is it the doctor you are listening to, or her?' Wren jerked his head in my direction, contempt in his eyes.

Dr Carlton bristled. 'Miss Wright may have been the first person to comment upon it, but it was I who carried out the review, and my clinical position stands.'

Mary added her two-pennyworth. 'Jennie has only ever had Race's best interests at heart.'

I wished they would be quiet. With every word they said they made it seem more and more as if the situation was of my making, when in fact it had nothing to do with me.

It had been Doug, not me, who had queried their motives. I had been clear there was no chance they could get Race to write a new will, but seeing the expression on Wren's face, I knew he would never believe me.

'Shouldn't Race decide whether we stay or not?' Although her question was addressed to everyone, Kira glared at me alone. Clearly she hoped pointing out that it was their uncle's house could stop their eviction.

'Actually, no,' Mr Landon interjected. 'It's my decision. You see, when Race got married his wife bought the house from him.' He turned to face Kira. 'You may not be aware of this but the estate was in very poor condition before the wedding, and it was Susan's money that allowed him to stay here, and for them to set up their various businesses. I believe he and your father fell out over the sale.'

As the solicitor spoke, Wren's clenched fists and Kira's ashen face demonstrated they had indeed not known this.

'Anyway, when she died, Susan left Race a life interest in everything, but on his death it will all pass to her family as that is where the money came from in the first place. I have made it my business to ensure Race is well cared for, but my clients are the actual owners of Great Haddows, and they decide who lives here.'

Wren leaped to his feet. 'Fine. We'll be out by the end of the week!'

'That won't be necessary.' The solicitor could afford to be magnanimous now he had won. 'Susan's family do understand that it may take a couple of weeks for you to arrange flights back to South Africa.'

'Who said anything about South Africa?' Wren enunciated his words carefully and stared directly at Mr Landon. 'We may stay in Kent.'

I could tell from his reaction that this was not the response the solicitor had expected or wanted, but he merely nodded his head and smiled as the two South Africans left the room.

I hurried after them, leaving the others to conclude the meeting. I had to let them know I had known nothing about the meeting and that I had not said their presence upset Race.

I heard them talking in the kitchen and, peeping through the crack between the open door and its frame, I saw Wren had his arms around his sister, trying to comfort her.

'I didn't upset him,' Kira was saying. 'I know I'm not the greatest nurse and admit I resented the fact that he lived while Dad and Mum died, but I didn't upset him. I wouldn't.'

'I know, sis, you don't have to try and convince me. It's that blasted Jennie who caused all this.'

I shivered at the venom in his voice.

'She may have made it all up, but it's my fault they believed her! If I hadn't been so pugnacious about how awful Race's life is and how if it were mine I'd want to die, no one would have paid her any attention.'

'Oh, I don't know, I think they've been looking for a reason to get rid of us for a long time. Anyway, we've nothing to fear and we're not finished yet. Wasn't it you who said she was so green it would be easy to pull the wool over her eyes?'

I didn't wait to hear any more.

I had intended to apologise to them and tell them what had really happened, but hearing them discuss me in that fashion, knowing they meant to try and trick me in some way, dissolved any guilt I might have felt and made me question whether in fact their leaving wasn't for the best after all. As far as I was concerned, anyone who set out to scam someone else wasn't worth bothering about — and hadn't I heard them planning to do just that, to me, with my own ears?

Wren disappeared to London the next morning and didn't return for three days, so I was spared coming face to face with him.

Kira and I avoided one another, any vestige of the friendship I had sought completely gone, so it wasn't until the day they moved out that I finally saw them.

Kira ignored me and wheeled her case to the waiting taxi, while her brother stood in front of me in the hall and blocked my way so I had no escape.

'Pleased with yourself, are you?' he demanded.

'I don't know what you're talking about.'

'Yeah, right! Well just think on this, my girl — if these tactics can be used on us, they can just as easily be used on you, and you'll now be alone in the house. Feel safe, do you?'

His words chilled me as nothing else had. Was he threatening me? Surely not!

Wren might not have lived up to my casting of him as a knight in shining armour, but I couldn't believe him a rogue, either. Rightly or wrongly I thought that if he truly were bad, I would sense it in some way. Or was it simply that I still fancied him in spite of everything, and believed I wouldn't feel that way if he were unscrupulous? But I knew women were duped by ruthless men all the time.

Later I was to bitterly regret being so gullible.

★　★　★

It was quiet in the house over the next few days. I hadn't thought I'd had much contact with Wren and Kira when they were living at Great Haddows, but when they went I realised it had been greater than I thought, for I seemed very alone.

Somehow all the latent fears I'd had when I first arrived resurfaced, and I jumped at every bump in the night or water-pipe groan, making sleep diffi-cult. The truth was I wasn't happy being on my own, the sole carer for Race overnight.

And following my exchange with Wren, my imagination ran riot. I was glad it was summer with long, light evenings, but feared how I would cope when winter came.

It was on a Friday night that I realised there was someone else in the house. It was coming up to midnight on a particularly dark evening, and I had been tossing and turning in bed, unable to get to sleep. I had seen a TV programme about insomnia which recommended getting up and going downstairs in such situations so the body doesn't become accustomed to the idea that beds are places where you lie awake.

But I was much too nervous to do that. I turned the bedside lamp on but clamped my eyes shut in a doomed attempt to drop off.

That was when I heard it: footsteps underneath me in the hall.

At first I told myself it was simply my

imagination playing tricks on me, but the more I listened, the more convinced I became that there was someone else in the house other than Race and myself.

Terror overtook me, and for a long while I lay rigid under the duvet, too scared to move.

Then I thought of Race. I was here to protect him and shivering in my bed wouldn't help.

I went to the door and shouted at the top of my voice, 'Who's there?'

I didn't expect a reply and got none, but I hoped that realising someone was awake in the house would frighten the intruder and encourage them to leave. I strained to listen, trying to catch the sound of someone retreating, but in all honesty all I could hear was the thumping of my own racing heart.

After five minutes I slipped across the landing to Race's room and turned on his light. He was fast asleep, looking as peaceful as ever, and I quickly flicked the switch off and left him.

I didn't want to go downstairs even though now, with my light on, I couldn't be sure that I had heard anyone at all, so I sat up in bed and read, ears acutely conscious of any sound, until finally I was too exhausted to keep my eyes open any longer and fell asleep in spite of myself.

* * *

Next morning I was even less sure that there had been an intruder and wondered whether what I had heard had simply been the normal creaking of floorboards that occurred in old houses.

I whisked through the morning routine and then went to investigate. There was no sign of any night-time visitors, and I felt something of a fool.

'Did you have a good night?' Mary asked as she cooked breakfast for Race.

'OK,' I replied, not wanting to let on about how scared I had been, but I noticed she gave me a funny look. Perhaps she had seen my light on in the early hours of the morning.

I was determined not to give in to night terrors that evening and went around checking the locks on every door and window. The front and back doors were fitted with bolts as well as mortice locks, but the door from the library to the patio was not.

I probably had seen too many films where detectives managed to get into locked rooms by wriggling the key out of the lock on the other side and pulling it through on a piece of strategically placed paper, so I removed the key and placed it on the table in the middle of the room. Then I pushed a heavy antique brass spittoon in front of the door and pulled all the curtains in the room so the trap I had set couldn't be seen. If someone tried to enter that way, I'd hear about it!

Whereas I had felt quite gung-ho while setting up 'the trap' I was less sanguine when the light faded and I went up to bed.

Race was fast asleep — he was rarely

awake even during the day now — and after making sure he was all right I went across the hall to my suite of rooms. I could lock my bedroom door, though I never had, but the door from the dressing-room to the passageway didn't even have a bolt on it. After that first evening I hadn't really worried about it, but tonight I pushed the wooden linen bin in front of it. It wouldn't prevent anyone entering if they wanted to — it wasn't heavy enough — but it would make a bang which would wake me up.

I sat up in bed trying to read a thriller — probably not the best choice of book when nervous — but as I found it impossible to concentrate and didn't take in more than one word in ten, it didn't affect my mood. Truthfully, I was so nervous I doubt anything could have made me more so.

Eventually I found it impossible to continue to force myself to stay awake, reached out to make sure I knew exactly where on the bedside table I'd put the torch I'd brought up from the kitchen to check on Race without having to turn his light on, and settled down to sleep.

* * *

The crash from the falling spittoon rang out at two in the morning.

I sat up in a trice, heart racing, panting with fear. Someone was in the house! What should I do? Having set the trap, I had no idea how to manage the situation. *Think, Jennie, think!*

Somehow, I forced my frozen legs to move and climbed out of bed to grab my mobile where I had left it charging on the dressing-table. I'd phone the police . . . but wait . . . we were miles from the nearest police station so it would take them ages to get here — and I needed help right now!

Of course — I could call Mary. I hadn't wanted to tell her my fears before because I had thought she'd think me childish and disapprove of my excessive security, but now I had been proved right — the crashing of the spittoon on the floor meant there definitely was someone trying to get into the house so there was no reason to remain silent any more.

With trembling fingers, I hit the speed dial for her number, peeping out of my window from behind the curtain to check whether I could see anyone on the patio below.

It was dark out with little moon, and I couldn't make out anything beneath me, but I was surprised to see that there was a light on in the cottage. At least that meant someone was awake — hopefully Mary, as that would mean my call wouldn't shock her awake.

The beam from inside her glazed front door shone out towards the orchard, and as I watched it seemed to me that I could see someone moving through the trees. Someone tall and well-built and in black from head to toe.

In that light I couldn't be sure and rushed next door to Kira's old room which gave a better view. I stared out of the latticed window, but if ever there had been anyone there he or she was long gone.

'Jennie?' Mary had recognised my number on her phone. 'What on earth are you ringing for at this time of night?'

'Someone's broken in!' I gasped and proceeded to tell her what had happened.

'We'll be right over!' she said and hung up.

I hurried into Race's bedroom and, realising I'd left the torch in my room, used the one on my mobile. He was lying on his side and snoring. Thank goodness he hadn't been disturbed by the noise! Then I remembered I had double-locked all the doors and rushed downstairs to undo the bolts so Mary would be able to get in when she used her kitchen keys. Normally I didn't bother with the bolts so that she didn't have a problem when arriving for work in the morning.

I didn't know if the intruder had left the library door unlocked, so taking a deep breath, I went in there to check. The key was still on the table, but the door was wide open. I went to shut it and was shocked to find someone outside.

I screamed.

Mary and Brian, both in their pyjamas and dressing-gowns, walked in.

'There, there, Jennie,' Mary waddled over to me in her slippers, 'You're overwrought.'

I was shaking from head to toe and unable to think straight. I sat down heavily on one of the two leather chairs that flanked the magnificent fireplace and began to cry. I really didn't want to show such weakness in front of them, but it seemed all my fears had come together and I felt completely powerless.

'Brian, get her a cup of tea,' ordered Mary, and then she sat opposite me and asked me to explain what was wrong.

Between muffled sobs I filled her in on all that had happened, including the fact that I had been too embarrassed to admit to her how frightened I had been.

When I'd finished she gave me a condescending smile and said I should never have kept my feelings to myself.

'If we'd known we'd never have left you here alone with Mr Race,' she said. 'I'll stay with you for the rest of the night, and then we'll speak to Mr Landon about arranging something on a more permanent basis.'

'I don't understand how he got in,' I said. 'I'm sure I locked the door.'

'Are you, Jennie?' Mary gave me a hard stare. 'You've been very emotional and it's an old lock. Don't you think you might have thought you did so when in fact you left it open?'

The strength drained out of me. Could I have done so? Had I been so keen to remove the key from the lock that I had omitted to check it really was locked?

'I suppose it's possible,' I said, 'but how would the intruder have known?'

'Luck,' she replied, 'Probably just a local lad with his eye on the main chance.'

I felt such a fool and stared unseeing at the fireplace. I didn't often go into the library as I had no reason to, and anyway, Kira had hogged it and I hadn't wanted to disturb her.

Brian brought me my tea and had put so much sugar in it that the taste quite shocked me out of my tears.

'We ought to call the police,' I said.

If I was going to be staying at Great Haddows I wanted to be sure the authorities knew what was going on.

'Oh, I don't think Mr Landon would want us to bother them,' Mary broke in. 'It's not as if anything has been taken, and the trouble with the police is they spend hours going over everything and I don't think Mr Race could take it.'

'But surely they ought to know that — '

'Really, there's no need. They're frightfully overstretched as it is, so to call them out to a minor event like this would be wrong.'

Brian indicated his agreement, so I

said no more. I still felt the incident should be reported but I had no more fight left in me.

'I'll take my tea to bed with me, if you don't mind,' I said, determining to throw it down the sink once I was alone, and Mary nodded.

'Now, don't forget, if you have any concerns at all in the night, just come to me. I'll sleep in Kira's old room.'

I nodded my thanks and retraced my steps upstairs.

I was sure I would never be able to sleep again, but once cocooned in my duvet, exhaustion overtook me.

7

Mary was as good as her word and had contacted Mr Landon to tell him about the night's events.

'He was shocked,' she said, 'and said we must get someone else to sleep in with you. As I told you, we used to have local girls waiting to go to university, but sadly I don't know of any now, and anyway, I'm not sure having two young girls together would be much use.'

She stressed the words *young girls* as if I were a silly teenager making a fuss about nothing.

I didn't understand her. One moment she was all concern and kindness, the next she was putting me down.

'However, I've got good news,' she rushed on. 'Doug Edwards happened to speak to Brian today, and when he heard what had happened, he volunteered to come and sleep here until we can make a more permanent arrangement. You like him, don't you? He tells me he's a light sleeper. And he's a very well-mannered young man, so there's nothing to worry about.'

I wasn't sure how I felt about this.

On the one hand he was someone I liked and felt I could trust, on the other hand if, as I suspected, he had taken a shine to me and hoped we might become close, was it such a good idea for him to move into the same house as me?

I didn't worry that he'd try and force his attentions on me, but he might get the wrong end of the stick and think my agreeing to such an arrangement meant I felt more for him than I did. Not that I'd had much say in the matter.

'He's going to come over tonight and will have Wren's old room at the end of the corridor, close to both you and Race.'

I nodded my understanding. If it was a choice between being alone in the house with Race or being with Doug,

I'd choose the latter any day.

I would just have to make it plain to him that I only wanted to be friends. Thinking of him reminded me of the kiss we had shared and how I had wished I could feel as alive in his arms as I had when dancing with Wren. Then I had hoped Wren might feel something for me — but there was no chance of that, now he thought I had betrayed him and Kira.

Kira . . . I worried about her and wished that our budding friendship hadn't been so completely extinguished. She was an enigma. I still wondered why she had forced herself into our set at the barn dance. What had that been all about?

Thinking about Wren made me feel sad.

I hated the idea that he thought I had reported him and Kira to Mr Landon, when in fact it had been nothing to do with me.

I supposed they were planning to return to South Africa, and the knowledge that I would probably never see him again gave me a horrid ache in my stomach which I didn't want to investigate.

★ ★ ★

Doug arrived that night and proved the perfect gentleman. Mary had made a shepherd's pie for us to share and we played cards after we'd stacked the dishwasher.

I took the opportunity to ask him about the decision that Wren and Kira should leave.

'I didn't say a word to anyone,' he assured me. 'I know what you told me was in confidence.'

'It did make me feel rather guilty after our conversation.'

'Well, it shouldn't, it was nothing to do with either of us, and it was for the best. Race doesn't need avaricious relatives circling him like buzzards.'

I noticed he referred to my employer with the same easy familiarity as all of us now, having dropped his usual polite use of his title. Only Mary insisted on still calling him *Mr* Race.

I couldn't allow his comment to pass.

'I really don't think they were — avariciously circling, I mean,' I quoted.

'Then why did they stay so long? Their parents were buried months ago and I can't see any other reason for them to be here.'

I didn't feel I could tell him what Kira had said about the crash. After all, it was only a suspicion on her part and was very likely untrue. She might want to find a reason for her parents' accident, but the reality was that bad things happened all the time to the nicest people.

'Kira is very lost and wants to feel she belongs somewhere,' I said, but Doug just pulled a face.

'She ought to grow up. She has family in South Africa and had never known any relatives here. Added to which, she's never made any attempt really to care for Race.'

'How do you know?' I was quite startled by his vehemence.

'Brian's been a friend for a long time.'

And they say men don't gossip! But I said nothing.

I was a little on edge when it came to bedtime but I needn't have worried. When I went upstairs Doug said he'd check all the doors and would watch the news on TV before retiring, so there were no awkward moments parting on the stairs.

The next morning he was gone before Mary arrived, so I was able to relax. I had worked hard at making sure he realised I only wanted to be a friend, and he seemed to have got the message.

* * *

Mary sent me into Dawston to do some shopping for her in the afternoon, and I was just coming out of the supermarket when I ran slap bang into Kira.

'How lovely to see you!' I said, not giving her time to berate me. 'Would you like to go for a coffee somewhere?'

She hesitated, and I could see she wanted to say no and storm off, but she was also a lonely girl in a foreign land, and it was that which got the better of her.

'OK,' she said, 'but only because I want to hear how Race is.'

We went to the local tearoom, an old-fashioned place in the midst of so many fast coffee outlets, but it was quieter there and we would be able to talk.

'Where are you staying?' I asked once we had settled down.

'In a bed and breakfast by the station,' she said. 'Wren can catch the train to London easily from there.'

'And you — are you still at the library?'

'Yes, though I'm thinking of going to work at Glandings, the auctioneer's in the high street. It's one of the companies Race and Susan used to run, though I don't know who does now.'

'Are you interested in antiques?'

She shrugged. 'Not especially, but I thought it might be interesting.'

'Do they sell houses, too? I suppose that would be more up your line.'

'Why?' she looked surprised.

'Well, I mean, because of your wanting to be an architect,' I said.

'Oh, yes,' she agreed, 'there is that.'

This was hard going.

'Have you got any further with your investigations into your parents' crash?' I asked by way of trying to make conversation.

'No. No one's interested, leastways, not round here. There is someone Wren met in London . . . ' She stopped as if she'd already said too much.

I smiled inanely, unsure how to respond. I felt sorry for her with all her conspiracy theories, but self-preservation meant I didn't forget her and Wren talking about me disparagingly and saying they could pull the wool over my eyes.

The waitress brought our drinks and the two cakes we had chosen. I waited until Kira had her mouth full before saying my piece; I didn't want to be interrupted.

'Kira, I want you to know that I didn't have anything to do with Mr Landon deciding he wanted you to leave. I certainly never suggested that you and Wren were bad for Race.'

Her expression showed she didn't believe me, but she said nothing.

'I had to tell Mary about the pills, you know that — but I never said that you had a bad effect on your uncle.'

Still silence. I had wanted her to listen to me but had expected a response eventually.

'You said you wanted to know how Race was. Well, he's OK, but . . . well, someone tried to break into Great Haddows a couple of nights ago.'

That caught her attention.

'What happened?'

'There was an intruder in the library. Whoever it was didn't get away with anything because I'd positioned a brass spittoon in front of the door which made a dreadful noise crashing over when the door was opened.'

'That was brave of you — or stupid.'

'It certainly wasn't brave. I was terrified, actually. But I managed to ring Mary and Brian and they came over. Unfortunately, we didn't catch the perpetrator.'

'What did the police say?'

I pinched my lips together before replying. 'They didn't — Mary and Brian felt there was no need to trouble them.'

'Race's house was broken into and they didn't think it should be reported?'

Her reaction was just what mine had been, but I had become more used to the idea now.

'Well, nothing was actually taken . . .'

'That's not the point. Race is a frail old man — a *rich* frail old man — and the only person he's got to protect him is you!'

'I do my best . . .' I wasn't going to let her send me on a guilt-trip.

'Oh, I'm not getting at you — it sounds as if you saved the day, actually — but it's ridiculous not to tell the police about the break-in. Aren't you scared to be there on your own?'

I'm not — on my own, I mean. Mary has arranged for Doug to sleep in Wren's old room, so we're quite safe.'

I knew I sounded defensive and wondered why.

Kira raised her eyebrows and watched me for a moment, saying, 'He's wheedled his way in?'

I didn't know what she meant. 'I don't know about wheedled. It's just a temporary arrangement until Mr Landon said gets someone in. It's very good of Doug.'

'Ah, the saintly Doug,' she mocked. 'Well let's hope he's as virtuous as you seem to think.'

Was she jealous? I wondered. Was that why she had gate-crashed our set at the barn dance? Had she wanted to dance with him all the time and been annoyed that he had invited me? It would make sense of her reaction now.

'I'm not going out with him, you know,' I explained, thinking it might make her feel better. 'We're just friends.'

'If you say so.' But her face told me she didn't believe me.

I had to know. 'Have you booked your flights back to South Africa?'

'Why, are you keen to get rid of us?'

I hoped my face wasn't giving the game away. 'Just making conversation,' I said, but my question effectively stopped all further discussion.

She stood up to go.

'Maybe we could meet again?'

Now why did I say that? I had nothing more to tell her and she had made it plain she didn't want to talk to me. But I didn't want to let her — or them — go.

'Maybe.'

And she was gone without a backward glance and without leaving me details of her new address.

* * *

'I hear you were in The Horn Of Plenty with Kira today,' Doug said to me that evening as we sat eating supper in the kitchen. 'Did she tell you their plans?'

'Not really, and anyway, how do you know what I was doing?'

I made a joke of it, but I wasn't very happy that he was aware of my movements. One heard about obsessive men who imagined they had been thwarted in love and started stalking the object of their desire. I hoped Doug wasn't one of them.

His response told me I had nothing to worry about. 'My mate works in Dawston and saw you two together,' he said. 'Actually, he works at Glandings, and he says Kira's applied for a job there. Did she mention anything about it to you?'

'She did, actually, though I don't know how serious she is.'

I was relieved that Doug's knowledge had come about as a result of chatting to a friend, rather than anything more sinister. I realised how stretched my nerves must be even to imagine he might have arranged to have me tailed. It was too ridiculous!

Yet that was the effect that living at

Great Haddows, with its underlying feeling of malaise, was having on me and I did wonder how long I would be able to bear it.

'Why do you say that?'

'Well, when I spoke to her she didn't seem to have much clue about the business, even though they sell houses, and she wants to be an architect.'

'Does she?'

'She was always reading about the houses in Haddows, mostly the older ones, I think.'

'She enjoys looking over old houses?' Doug looked interested. 'Did she do so here?'

I thought for a moment. 'Not that I noticed, but then, she was almost always holed up in the library, reading.'

Doug stretched extravagantly. 'I wonder if an old place like this has any secrets,' he said, 'you know, like a hidden room or something. Did Kira ever mention anything like that?'

'No, she said very little to me at all, if I'm honest. But I suppose there might be something — a priest-hole, perhaps — this house is about the right age. I've seen a date somewhere that says fifteen-ninety, though I can't remember where — is it above the entrance?'

He frowned. 'I don't think so. I'm sure Kira once told Brian the house was built in the early fifteen-hundreds. Tell me more about priest-holes.'

I racked my brains to dredge up what I had learned at school. My class had been taken on a school outing to Oxborough Hall, a beautiful moated country house in Norfolk, chock-full of fascinating objects, but once I had seen it, all I could focus on was the brick-built priest-hole. It had been so small and confining, and the thought that a man had hidden there, totally at the mercy of others, had rather spoilt the day for me.

'Well, I think it was after the Babington plot — you know, when supporters tried to free Mary Queen of Scots from her captivity and place her on the English throne. When that failed, a law was passed making it illegal for

Catholics to celebrate Mass, and to overcome this many grand houses built hiding places for their priests.'

'I wonder if the Engletons did,' Doug said.

'Well, if its location hasn't been handed down through the generations it's unlikely we'll ever find out now. They were very well disguised.'

'You're right, of course.' He gave a rueful grin, then added, 'Did Kira say anything about returning to South Africa?'

'I asked her but she wasn't forthcoming.'

'It seems odd, the way they're hanging around. Their parents died months ago and I'd have expected them to go by now.'

I decided I could tell him a little.

'I think they want to clear up some lose ends about the car crash. I'm not exactly sure what, but they want to make sure everything is properly sorted out.'

'I thought it already had been. The only problem is, they don't want to accept it.'

'I understand they have the ear of someone in London . . . '

For some reason I didn't want Doug to think they were simply being pig-headed. This captured his attention and he frowned.

'Well, good luck to them, but it won't change anything. Mary's never actually said this, but she saw Kira's parents drive off on the day they died, and she said Paul was driving like a madman.'

I hadn't heard there had been a witness to his driving — that did put a different complexion on things. I supposed the housekeeper hadn't told Wren and Kira because she didn't want to upset them. How much harder it would be to bear their parents' death if they knew it had definitely been their father's fault.

Doug cleared the table while I went to settle Race for the night.

'I'll make you a hot drink when you get back.'

He was proving to be remarkably well house-trained, and I had been pleased to discover I didn't need to trail around picking up after him.

It was sheer luck that I had my mobile in my pocket in Race's room — I hadn't been very successful in my quest to remember to keep it with me as so few people called me, and really I used its other functions more than the phone facility — so I jumped when it rang.

'Jennie?' I recognised his voice at once and my heart skipped a beat. 'Can you talk?'

'Yes.'

Foolishly pleased to hear Wren's voice, I still didn't forget that the last time we had spoken I had questioned whether he was warning me off.

'Kira's just told me about the house being broken into. Are you OK?'

I was absurdly pleased he appeared concerned.

'I'm fine,' I said. 'Let me go to my bedroom. I'm with Race at the moment.'

I padded over to my room and sat on my bed.

'I don't think you should be there alone,' he barked. 'Why don't you look for another job?'

Just as quickly as my spirits had raised they plummeted down again as I grasped that it wasn't concern for my welfare that had prompted the call, but a wish to get rid of me.

'I'm not alone.' I hoped I'd put a cold enough chill in my voice. 'Doug is staying over.'

'Doug? There? Just the two of you?'

He sounded aghast. Clearly Kira hadn't fully briefed him. Perhaps she had thought Doug moving in had been a temporary arrangement.

'The two of us and Race.'

I purposely put the emphasis on his uncle's name. I didn't know what his beef was, but the reason I was there at all was for Race, and it seemed to me he wasn't considering that.

It appeared to give him pause for thought.

'Can we meet up to discuss this?' he asked.

'I don't think we have much to say.'

Much as I'd have loved to have seen him, my first duty was to Race, and if Wren wanted me to leave I wasn't interested in talking to him.

'Do you remember I once said to you that things aren't as they seem? That I was working behind the scenes? I'd like to tell you about what I'm doing, if you're willing to meet.'

My head was telling me it would be much safer to refuse and hang up, but my heart was having none of it.

'OK, but you'll have to come here.'

Cautious, I knew, but such odd things had been happening I didn't want to go somewhere strange.

'You're forgetting Mr Landon. Mary and Brian would be sure to report me if I turned up at Great Haddows.'

'No problem — they've got some do to attend in London tomorrow and won't be back until late, and as Doug is working late he's agreed to fetch them from the station and bring them home, so he'll be out, too. Why not pop over early evening? Race will be in bed so there's no chance of you catching him unawares, and if he doesn't see you, I don't see how Mr Landon could say you had made him agitated, do you?'

'OK. I'll see you then — and Jennie . . . ' He paused. 'Please be careful.'

A warm glow came over me as I pocketed my mobile. He was concerned for my welfare — how surprising was that!

I tried to damp down the fizzy excitement that bubbled up inside me but only succeeded in pressing my clenched hands to my mouth and giving a delighted smile.

It didn't seem foolish at that point to invite him to come to the house when I would be totally alone apart from a frail old man. My instinct told me he was a good man . . . and instinct had never let me down before.

★   ★   ★

I saw the Kents set off in Doug's car in the morning and spent the rest of the day wondering about what Wren wanted to tell me.

I also took quite a long time getting ready for his arrival — washing my hair, choosing which clothes would best look as if I had casually put them on when I got up and not taken hours to decide what showed me to best advantage, and applying a little more make-up than usual.

I chatted to Race about what I'd decided throughout the day, sad that he no longer engaged with me in any way, but hopeful that Wren would have come up with something to help him.

At nine o'clock I heard the roar of a motorbike up the drive, and a tall, muscular biker all dressed in black, right down to the visor, alighted and strode to the front door. The costume epitomised his stance as the pack leader — a bad boy with a heart of gold as I fondly cast him.

I opened the door and hoped he

wouldn't notice how quickly I was breathing.

He removed his helmet as he entered the house. 'As I haven't the use of the estate car any more,' he said by way of explanation, 'I hired the bike.'

'It suits you,' I replied, and we walked on into the kitchen.

It was my favourite room in the house, large and homely, all stripped pine and gleaming appliances with the Aga in the corner. I made us both a coffee and waited for him to tell me what he wanted.

'Kira's told you that we both doubt Dad's car crash was an accident,' he began. 'And I approached a private investigator to look into it for me. As luck would have it he was an ex-policeman, just retired from the Met, so he had lots of inside knowledge.'

'About what — a car crash in Kent?'

'Not exactly — about Susan and Race.' He sighed heavily for a moment, as if weighed down by what he was about to tell me. 'You know Landon said that Race and my father fell out over Race's marriage?'

I nodded.

'Well, it wasn't so much about the wedding, it was about what happened afterwards.

'You see it was true the estate was very run down, and although Race was the elder brother, Dad was running it. Race was never interested in the place except as a bolt hole because he was drawn to the bright lights and wanted to have fun. He wanted to spend what little money there was left on himself, while Dad wanted to make a go of things here. And then Race met Susan.'

'Didn't your father like her?'

'I don't think liking her had anything to do with it. Now I've had a chance to speak to Inspector Day, he told me about her and her family, and I can see exactly why Dad would have wanted to get away. You see, he was always straight as a die, it was something he felt very strongly about and which he impressed upon Kira and me.

'Apparently, Susan wasn't just some

girl Race had met in London, she was the daughter of a crime baron who had reached the stage where he was looking for respectability, and he saw Race as the family's entrée into legitimacy.'

'Well, if he wanted to go straight — ' I began.

Wren interrupted me. 'No, no, he didn't, not really. What he was looking for was a reputable front he could hide behind. As he saw it, the Engletons were an old established family who, while no longer rich, were very well thought of. If Susan married Race, her father, Trevor Preston, could see a way to continue his unsavoury activities, hidden behind a highly regarded name.'

'And Paul didn't accept that?'

'No, he saw straight through it. Race did too, of course, but he didn't care. Remember I told you he was hedonistic in his youth? It seems he was happy enough to embrace his father-in-law's ways so long as he had access to the spoils.

'He and Susan began to set up all sorts of different companies, all of which appeared completely legitimate and were very successful, but the police always believed they were actually a front for money-laundering. They never had any proof, which was why Race and Susan were never prosecuted, but Dad sniffed corruption and when Race refused to back down, he emigrated to South Africa.

'It was dangerous to cross the Prestons and he wanted to live a life as far away from them as possible, completely free of their influence.'

'What happened then?' I was intrigued.

'That's the problem — no one really knows. I mean, it had gone on for years, and then Aunt Susan developed cancer and died. Soon afterwards Race wrote to Dad, which led to him and Ma flying over here post haste.

'He said he didn't want to talk to me about the letter until he had seen Race and gained a better understanding of what was going on, and he told me to be careful and to take care of Kira while they were away — which was an unusual thing for him to say. It was almost as if he sensed danger.'

He stood up and walked to the window to look out over the darkening fields.

'He phoned to say they had arrived all right and that Landon had arranged for them to stay here. Then the next thing we heard was that they had been involved in the car accident and that they had been killed.'

I could plainly see the enormity of the loss still affected him.

'And you came over for the funeral.' I completed the story.

'Yes. We meant to go straight back, but then I began to ask a few questions and things didn't seem as clear-cut as all that. We decided to stay a while and see what we could find out, which thus far hasn't been a lot. But now that I have ex-Inspector Day on side I feel more positive.'

'Well, your story has cleared up one thing for me — why I've always felt Great Haddows has this malign atmosphere. If it has housed criminal activity,

I'm not surprised.'

'You feel it too, do you? It affected Kira quite badly, and yes, according to Ron Day, the crimes were brutal. They may not have been played out here, but this was where all the decisions were made. And the police are still no nearer catching the criminals and putting a stop to it.

'The Prestons continue to control their family business because there is no proof of their wrong doing — they cover their tracks exceedingly well.'

I remembered something Kira had told me.

'The auctioneers, Glandings, they were owned by Susan and Race, weren't they?'

'Yes.' He nodded. 'And my daft little sister thought she might go and work there! I soon put her right on that! She's always been headstrong. She was sure she would find the answer to the riddle of why the Prestons chose Great Haddows as their main base in its history, which was why she read all those old books.

'When Mary started making comments about it she said she wanted to be an architect, which she doesn't; she hasn't the faintest idea about the subject!

'Anyway, when I told her what Inspector Day had said, she wanted to come back here and search for evidence of the Prestons' nefarious deeds because she said she hadn't looked at the many business records here, only the ones about the house. But I told her she couldn't.'

'That wouldn't be a good idea,' I agreed. I could just imagine what Mary would say if she caught her!

'Quite. However, I did wonder if you would allow me to do so sometime? You could let me know when the coast would be clear and — '

'Absolutely not!'

Was that the real reason he had come? To persuade me to act as his lookout while he ransacked Race's archives? I wondered if this Inspector Day was a real person — perhaps Doug had been right and Wren and Kira were trying to get something out of Race.

'I thought you'd say that. You can't imagine true evil, can you?' He fixed his green eyes on me and looked very serious. 'Jennie, you have to realise that this is not a game — these people are ruthless — you need to leave.'

'I can't desert Race.' As I said it I realised how strongly I felt about the situation. 'He's alone and frail and whereas Mary is very proper in her approach I don't think she actually likes him. Everybody deserves a little love in their life, even those who've done wrong in the past.'

'But it's not safe.'

'Brian and Doug are on hand, and even when the intruder got in he ran off the minute he realised he had been sussed.'

'But we don't know who can be trusted. Who's to say the Kents aren't part of the gang?'

I burst out laughing. 'Now that's a bit far-fetched! Can you honestly see Mary as an international criminal?'

'Landon hired her.'

'The solicitor? What's he got to do with it?'

'You heard him tell us he had been the financial advisor for Susan and Race for years,' he reminded me. 'Well, those years covered the period when it's believed they were actively involved in money laundering. And he said he still represents her family. There are crooked lawyers as well as straight ones, you know.'

I hadn't thought of that. But what would he or the Prestons have to gain by harming Race? He was hardly a threat to anyone these days. The coward in me wanted to run away . . . but Race needed me.

'I can't leave him,' I said, 'Mr Landon didn't hire Doug, and Doug offered to come here when he heard about the intruder.'

Wren punched his hand with his fist.

'You don't know the first thing about Doug, either,' he said. 'Kira tried to sound him out at the dance, but he wasn't giving anything away.'

'Is that why she gate-crashed our set?'

He looked at me for a moment before replying.

'One reason,' he said before changing the subject. 'Jennie, if you're determined to stay, promise me you'll be careful.'

I agreed I would and I made us each another coffee and then went to check on Race.

By the time I returned, it was getting late and I started to fret that Doug and the Kents might return before Wren had left.

'Don't worry, I'm off,' he said. 'Just remember what I've said.'

And he was gone.

I had just finished drinking my coffee when Doug came in. I'd intended to go straight to bed, but Doug was buzzing and wanted to chat.

'We can have a nice nightcap together,' he said, and nervous he shouldn't guess I had just been drinking with someone else, I forced a second cup down.

At last I was able to thankfully climb the stairs to bed where any worries that Wren's revelations would stop me sleeping were proved entirely false the moment my head touched the pillow.

8

For the first time since I'd been at Great Haddows I overslept the next day.

I had stopped setting my alarm as I'd got into the routine of waking early, so it was a shock to realise I was an hour late. I felt I ought to leap out of bed and race downstairs, but my body felt unnaturally floppy and my eyes didn't seem to want to open.

I pulled myself up and started to walk towards the en suite bathroom; my legs so heavy I imagined myself in concrete boots. As I passed the bedside-table I stumbled against it and the reading light fell to the floor.

It was an elegant hand painted Chinese lamp in blue and white porcelain, and if it hadn't been for the fact that it caught on the side of the bed frame as it fell, there would have been no damage at all. As it was, it was just my luck that the cracked neck caused the bulb and electrics to slip drunkenly to one side, but the footed vase remained intact.

Very carefully I picked it up and stuffed the bulb back into place. Well, it would be more truthful to say I balanced it, actually, but unless you looked very closely, you wouldn't have known it was broken. I determined to come back to it and see what I could do to fix it when I felt more myself.

I finally surfaced downstairs at nine-thirty. I was worried what Mary would say, but she was quite sanguine about it.

'It's been a worrying time for you, so I didn't wake you,' she said. 'I've seen to Race, so sit down and have a cup of tea and some toast.'

In fact, the last thing I wanted was anything as dry as toast. My mouth felt as if I had been in a desert for months, and all I wanted was fresh orange juice. I was worried I might be sickening for something — perhaps the same bug that had laid Mary low — but as the day progressed I began to feel more normal and wondered why I'd had such a strange reaction.

I decided I had better try and repair the bedside lamp before Mary found it, and having checked that Race was all right, I carried it to my bed and inspected the cracked neck.

The bulb fitting fell out in my hands, and as it did so, I saw there was something white below it in the body of the vase. It looked like a paper scroll. I slipped my fingers down inside to try and reach it but it was too far down, and when I turned the lamp upside-down the mysterious paper remained resolutely stuck in place.

Never one to give up easily, I took my tweezers from my make-up bag and by dangling them down the neck was just able to grab a corner of the paper and pull it out.

Carefully I unrolled it, and saw it was a copy of a type-written letter. It wasn't the original because it wasn't signed, and it was addressed to Mr Paul Engleton in South Africa.

When I realised what I had, I froze.

Race had made a copy of the letter he had sent his brother, and then had placed it in the lamp. But why? He kept meticulous records downstairs, so why hadn't he just filed it away?

The answer rose unbidden — because he knew it would be destroyed if he didn't. What was it he had been scared of?

With trembling hands, I straightened the scroll and began to read . . .

Dear Paul

I sincerely hope this reaches you but you may have moved, so I must just pray that if you have, the South African post office service can find you.

You'll be surprised to hear from me again after all these years, and I know you said you wanted nothing more to do with me, but you were always a good man and I think you will want to help.

You were right to get away when you did. I thought I could play the system and not get burned, but life isn't like that. Once you've crossed a certain line, there's no way back.

My darling Susan got leukaemia and passed away last year, but before she died she made me promise to put things right.

I must do that, Paul. But I'm pretty sure they're on to me, so I have to watch myself as that's the last thing they'd allow. They daren't kill me while I have what they want, but I've learned from them that there are other ways of controlling a man and I'm afraid of what they might try to do.

You're my nearest relative and we were close once, and sometimes they use relations to get back at people they want to pull into line. I don't know if you have a family, but if you have, you need to protect them.

They won't harm me until they get what they want, and I'm not going to give it to them, but I think time is running out for me.

So what I'm asking — begging — you to do, is to come back to Great Haddows to help me right a great wrong.

The last thing you said to me was that I'd tarnished the Engleton name. Please give me the chance to salvage it.

Your loving brother,
Race

The hairs on my arms were standing on end as I read the letter.

This meant that everything Wren had suspected was true. But it also meant that he and Kira were in danger and I had to warn them!

Then I thought that I was in danger too if they found out I had read this letter!

But who were 'they'? I had no idea, and Race didn't say. I assumed Susan's father had died some years ago, so who had stepped into his shoes and what did they want from Race now?

I needed to hide the letter. It was important no one discovered Race had made a copy.

It seemed more and more likely to me that the Engletons' crash had not been an accident, and if that was so, it was very probable that 'they' must have found and destroyed the original letter. If the contents were considered so incendiary, it was vital that I hid the copy carefully until I could give it to Wren or the police.

But where? There was too great a chance that the broken lamp would be discovered, and if it was, so would any scroll inside it, so I couldn't return it to its original hiding place.

Under the mattress, behind a picture, in my make-up bag, all the usual places were too obvious. Then I had what I hoped was a brilliant thought . . .

Race's letter implied that the dreaded 'they' had been looking for months for something they believed he had, and presumably they had stripped his bedroom bare to find it. If they had already searched in there with a fine tooth comb, they were unlikely to do so again. Ergo, until I could hand it over, that would be the safest place to keep it.

I crept across the landing and slipped into Race's room. Slumped in his armchair, he didn't open his eyes. On the far wall was a wide bookcase and I removed a particularly obscure-looking volume and placed the letter in the middle. Then I pushed the book back into place and tiptoed out.

★   ★   ★

Next day, nervous as I was, I had to phone Wren, so I went for my usual lunchtime stroll and made my way to the far side of the garden. Since Wren had called me I had his number on my mobile, and I hit speed dial. After three rings voicemail cut in, and as I hadn't prepared anything, I wasn't sure what to say. I didn't want to be too explicit.

'Hi Wren, it's Jennie. Could you call me, please? I've something important to discuss.'

He rang that evening, eager to hear what I had learned, but I wouldn't say anything over the phone and arranged for him to bike over to Great Haddows the next night when the Kents would again be out. They seemed suddenly to have developed quite a social life, which suited my purpose — especially as Doug was acting as their taxi driver for the second time.

'I'll stay in Dawston 'til their train gets in,' he told me. 'No point coming back here if I have to go out again soon afterwards.'

Wren roared up on his motorbike as the sun began to set.

'What was so secret that you couldn't tell me over the phone?' He removed his helmet and undid his leathers before sitting down.

'I found this.' I handed him the letter and left him to read it.

He skim-read it, glanced at me with wild eyes, and then read it again, taking longer to do so.

'Where was it?' he asked.

I told him about my slight accident and how the letter had been in the body of the lamp.

Wren frowned. 'So he knew they'd be looking for it and put it somewhere he thought it would be safe.'

'But why? Surely keeping a copy wasn't a safe thing to do at all.'

I knew if I had an incriminating letter, I'd burn it rather than risk someone finding it.

'And why hide it somewhere where the chances of it being found were very small?'

I didn't add that if I hadn't been so woozy, it would still be slumbering in the lamp, like Ali Baba's genie.

'Who knows what he was thinking when he hid it? The letter shows he was in a highly excitable state — worried for himself and his brother and family, yet fixated on carrying out his wife's last wish.'

'What will you do now?'

'Give it to Ron Day,' Wren said. 'He's still got links with the Force and will know the right people to involve.' He looked very determined. 'Jennie — you have to let me search the archives now we know there's something Race had that would bring down the Prestons.'

But I was too scared. The thought of violent gangsters watching Race terrified me.

'No, you must leave it to the police. If they haven't got what they want, they must still be looking, and I'm not going to do anything that might put Race in danger.'

But deep inside I worried that my fear was more for myself than for anyone else.

We argued then, with Wren telling me forcefully why it was important I let him into the study, and me refusing to be budged. While I am of a nervous disposition, I can also be very single-minded, and as I honestly thought it a bad idea, I refused to give in. At one point I thought he would explode, but he suddenly backed down and suggested he made us both a cup of coffee.

I was relieved he was more calm.

'I'll just check in on Race. All this talk about violent criminals has made me jumpy!'

I tried to laugh it off as a joke, but actually I was feeling quite frightened.

Race was sleeping the sleep of the just, and when I went back into the kitchen Wren was putting on his helmet.

'I just realised the time,' he said, 'I'd better be off before we get caught.'

He pointed towards the steaming drink he had left for me on the table. I nodded and smiled. He was right, of course, but I was terribly disappointed. I was sorry we had rowed and that I'd had to refuse him, and I didn't want him to go.

I didn't want him to go . . . that was the crux of the matter. There was something about this man that set my heart singing and over which I had no control. As I shut the door behind him I knew, without a shadow of a doubt, that

I had fallen in love with him.

The shock of this discovery turned my knees to water and I sat down at the table nursing the coffee he had made me and tried to make sense of it. How could I be in love with someone I barely knew — someone who had given no indication he felt anything for me at all, and with whom I seemed to argue more than laugh?

I didn't have long to meditate on my feelings because very shortly after Wren had left, Doug's car pulled up outside. I heard him bid good night to the Kents as I washed up my cup, and then he came into the kitchen.

'Hello, you still up? What about I make us both a cup of coffee?'

Not again, I thought. Truth to tell I was feeling pretty water-logged, but not wanting to appear stand-offish I nodded and he put the kettle on.

'We nearly had an accident just down the road,' he said as he spooned sugar into his cup. 'Some madman on a motorbike went thundering round the corner by the church. He was lucky I missed him.'

I gave a watery smile and hoped Doug couldn't sense my shock. Thank heavens Wren had left when he did.

'Did you get his registration number?'

'No, it was all over too quickly — don't know who it was. There aren't any bikers who live round here, I don't think.'

'I haven't heard of any,' I said and went to rummage in the cupboard, ostensibly for sweeteners, although I normally took sugar in coffee. I didn't want my face to give me away.

'Oh, I've already sugared you,' Doug said as I carried the saccharin to the table. I shrugged and shook my head to show it didn't matter.

'How's Race these days?' he asked. 'Any more agitation or gibberish?'

I didn't like him calling it 'gibberish'. I felt it demeaned Race somehow.

'He hasn't said anything else to me, if that's what you mean.'

My tone must have given me away.

'Sorry, didn't mean to sound hard. I haven't had much to do with people like him and don't know the correct terms.'

I did understand. If people didn't realise a term was offensive, I didn't see why they should be castigated for it, and at least Doug realised the word he had used was inappropriate.

'I just wondered if he'd given any clues as to what he's thinking?'

'Oh no, nothing like that,' I said, 'He's never been what you might call lucid.'

I managed to force the coffee down and then headed thankfully for bed, suddenly quite tired.

I switched off the light, sure I would be unable to sleep as I considered the enormity of my admission to myself about Wren.

* * *

I was wrong and the next thing I knew, the morning alarm on my mobile was sounding. I had started to use it after I had overslept.

In fact I hadn't needed it again until today, as I had reverted to waking naturally to the early morning birdsong. Unfortunately, my lack of technical prowess meant that, having set it to repeat, I had yet to work out how to cancel the instruction.

I reached out to pick up the mobile, patting across the whole of the bedside-table, only to discover it wasn't there. Wearily I sat up and saw it was playing its tune from the dressing room, so I hobbled across to turn it off and stumbled against the linen bin.

'Ouch!' I said aloud, rubbing my hip.

I wondered why the bin was facing the door diagonally. Most nights I pushed it firmly against the door to ensure no one could enter without my knowledge, but I had been so tired last night perhaps I'd forgotten to do so.

Just my luck that the one day I needed to be up early because it was Mary's day off and I had to get Race's breakfast, I should oversleep again. But at least the alarm had woken me, and I didn't feel as bad as I had on that last occasion. But it was clear that the stress of what was proving to be something of a cloak and dagger existence was getting to me.

Once Race had eaten all he wanted, which wasn't much these days as he tended to slump over his tray and fall asleep, I helped him into the bathroom.

Once safely ensconced I returned to tidy his bedroom and as I wiped down his furniture I came across the old book that had so agitated him when he was off his medication, still under the box of tissues. I doubted the sight of it would set him off these days, but nevertheless thought it best to remove it from his room.

I slipped into the hall and left it on the large oak chest there, ready to take downstairs.

Later I went to put it in the library, but when I entered the room I saw that the door to the study was slightly ajar and went to shut it.

What I saw as I looked into the room shocked me: there were open box files everywhere with papers strewn over the two desks!

Who on earth would have done this? No one ever went in there, except occasionally Mary to clean. She had told me that all the important papers had been removed by Mr Landon, so there was nothing in the room that could have interested anyone.

Then an awful thought struck me.

I remembered how insistent Wren had been that I should allow him to search the archives and how I had once feared I might have been wrong to trust him — that perhaps his Inspector Day did not exist. What had Kira said about pulling the wool over my eyes?

I had dismissed such suspicions when I realised I was in love with him, but what if my feelings for him were hiding the truth?

I thought back to his visits and the conversations we had had about the archives and then it hit me — on both occasions I had been absolutely pole-axed when I went to bed afterwards! Wren had had the opportunity to doctor my coffee!

It seemed so clear now — I had seen how drugs could adversely affect someone when Race had been on the wrong medication — and now I thought about it, the way I had felt when I had broken the lamp had not been normal.

But what was it that was so important to him that he would drug me and risk getting caught by Doug? Because whereas I had been drugged, Doug had not and could have easily heard someone moving about downstairs. And how had he got in? Had he kept a copy of one of the house keys when he left?

I knew Doug didn't bolt the doors when he locked up even though I'd have liked him to. He said it was so Mary could get in with her key when she needed to, but I suspected it was also because he didn't see it as particularly macho to double-lock everywhere when he was supposed to be protecting me.

I racked my brains as I tried to work out why Wren would risk everything by breaking in and then the awful idea dawned . . . who actually knew Kira and Wren Engleton? Race and their father had lost touch before they were born, and there'd been no contact until after Paul Engleton's death. What if the South African pair were not Paul's children but impostors — members of the Preston gang trying to find out whatever it was Race had hidden that could bring down a crime family?

I didn't doubt that some of what Wren had told me was true — not that Mr Landon was in cahoots with the gang, but certainly that Susan Engleton had been part of it and that Race had been sucked in — the letter to Paul proved that. Wren had had to give me some information to ensure I'd let him know if I found out anything else — but the bit that was the lie was his assertion that he and Kira were Race's nephew and niece. I had allowed myself to be convinced because they all shared the same bone structure and good looks — but that did not mean they were related. After all, I'd heard of children being told by friends who didn't know they were adopted how like their parents they looked.

My usual fear overwhelmed me. What should I do? Who could I trust?

If I called Mary I doubted she would accept what I said — she had such a touching belief in the arrangements made by Mr Landon and Dr Carlton that even though she didn't like Wren and Kira, she'd simply dismiss my concerns and say I must have left Wren alone long enough last night for him to rummage through the study. She wouldn't see the danger there.

But I knew there was danger. If someone was prepared to drug you they didn't have your best interests at heart — they had no idea how the medication would affect you — so they would only do it if the stakes were incredibly high.

If only I knew what Wren (or whoever he was) was looking for, I'd have more of an idea about what to do. But I couldn't do it alone — I wasn't brave enough. I decided to call Doug and ask him to come back to the house — he had given me good advice when he'd said to tell Mary about what the pharmacist had said, and together we could work out what to do.

I wondered where I'd left my phone and spent a frenzied ten minutes searched each room before I found it by Race's bed and hit redial.

* * *

'You mean to tell me you found a copy of this letter and *gave it to Wren?*'

I shrank as I heard the intense anger in Doug's voice. I couldn't blame him; of course, I had been a fool. I admitted I had and began to explain all that had happened.

'Wait!' he commanded. 'Don't tell me now, I'm coming right over and you can explain face-to-face.'

He arrived within three-quarters of an hour which gave me enough time to calm down and straighten out in my own mind what had happened, and when.

'This is just amazing!' He stared at me, wide-eyed with astonishment, when I'd finished. 'You mean Wren came here twice and wanted you to let him go through the archives?'

I nodded. 'Yes, but as I've said, I don't believe he is Wren. It's the only thing that makes sense. He may be working for the Prestons.

'You said you thought he and Kira wanted to persuade Race to change his will for them, but I think it was more than that. What if, after Paul's death, the Prestons arranged for them to come here and pose as Race's nephew and niece so they have access to the house and can search for whatever it is they need?

'We now know from the copy of the letter I found that Race was intending to go the police to 'put things right'. If he meant to go to the authorities with proof of the money-laundering or whatever it was they were doing, that would be worth an awful lot to the Prestons and also to anyone else who got their hands on it.'

'It does sound a bit fantastic.' I could see Doug was having trouble imagining such a thing.

'I know, but since I've thought about it I've been on social media and I can't find hide nor hair of Wren and Kira Engleton. If Paul really was afraid of the Preston family it would make sense that he'd make sure his children didn't broadcast to the world who they were and where they lived, and that of course, made it easier to turn up here and pretend to be them.'

I could see Doug was beginning to think my theory was not so outlandish after all.

'There's a couple of other things,' I said, warming to my subject. 'I've been thinking, I'm sure I locked the library when I set my trap, so whoever broke in had to have a key. And who was always in there, reading? Kira. She could easily have had a spare key cut and given it to her brother — if he is her brother.

'After the break-in I was sure someone was walking through the trees but I couldn't see properly in the darkness. The only thing I know is that the person was tall and dressed in black from head to toe.'

I paused as what that meant dragged me down.

'When Wren came here in his leathers and visor he was all in black. He told me he had only recently hired the motorbike, but he could just have likely have had it all the time.'

'We need to be careful we don't scare him off. Have you arranged to meet him again?'

'No! I don't want to put him in a position where he has power over me.'

'I understand your reasoning, but you mustn't withdraw or he'll realise something is wrong.'

He was right, of course, but I hated the thought that I'd have to continue my contact with Wren. The shock of realising how I had been duped had been great, but far worse was the awful ache in my heart whenever I thought about him. Because I was learning that knowing a person is bad does not stop you loving them — nor deluding yourself that 'the love of a good woman' could redeem a villain. How could I be so stupid and why did my heart contract when I had thought that he cared about me?

'What should I do?'

'Wait 'til he contacts you and then let me know at once what he wants,' he said, pointing his index finger at me and wagging it as he gave his instructions. 'I'll keep my mobile on all the time, so you'll always be able to get me.'

'OK,' I agreed with a heavy heart, 'But what will you do?'

'Don't you worry about that, you just make sure you keep me informed.'

For a moment his face clouded over

and I saw how angry he was with Wren and — stupid, stupid Jennie! — I was momentarily worried about what Doug would do to him. He must have seen my concern because he took my hand.

'Don't worry, Jennie,' he said, 'I'll make sure that you and Race are safe.'

9

The next few days dragged interminably. Doug had tidied up the study as he said he didn't want to upset Mary, so when she came back on duty I had to be careful not to say anything that might make her question what had happened during her time off.

Race remained as fatigued as ever which meant time played heavily on my hands and I found I was constantly on edge — torn between hoping Wren would ring, and wishing that he never would. I was worried that he would recognise there was something wrong from my voice — he had known there was at once when I'd found out he'd told Mary about my wanting to take Race outside, and I knew my happy childhood meant I was something of an open book. There had been no secrets in our house and my temperament meant I only enjoyed such adventures at one remove, in books.

He finally rang on Monday when I was alone in the house. By then I was feeling very tense though I did my best to hide it.

He dispensed with preliminaries and got straight to the point. 'Jennie, I've spoken to Day, and he really thinks you should get out. The Prestons are a nasty bunch and apparently after the old man died Susan's brother took over, and he's even worse! Day has taken the letter to his colleagues in the Met, and they're very interested. If it's true Race has hidden evidence somewhere and it could help them smash the gang.'

Oh, you are so plausible! I thought. 'I really can't leave Race. I need to protect him.' I didn't add *from you* but that was what I meant.

The thought of leaving that frail old man to Wren's tender ministrations didn't bear thinking about! I understood now why Kira had been so averse to caring for him — it hadn't been her despair at her parents' death that had turned her against him, rather her knowledge that he had the power to bring her family down.

'Don't be ridiculous — they're an incredibly nasty set of rogues and if they find out you've given that letter to me they'll be livid. And they'll be looking for whatever evidence Race put together which is very likely going to be somewhere at Great Haddows. They haven't found it yet, so you can bet they'll keep looking.'

I bet he would, too, and how much easier it would be if I wasn't there, always looking out for Race. I wouldn't have put it past him to have had someone in mind to replace me. If I left, Mary would have to advertise for someone new, and how easy for him to put his plant in the house. I might not let him in to search the archives, but his minion would.

'Meet me at Dawston Country Park at two o'clock — you could leave Race alone for an hour. You know he won't move.'

'No!'

I knew I couldn't see him. As long as I kept him at arm's length I could maintain my resolve, but I wasn't sure how strong I would be when he was standing next to me. I hoped I wouldn't give in — but I had never been in love before and who knew how I would react?

'I'll be waiting for you.'

He hung up before I could reply.

For one moment I was tempted to go, but then I thought of Race and knew I couldn't. And I really didn't trust myself. Safer by far to hang up and inform Doug, which was exactly what I did.

'Leave it to me. I'll be over by four and tell you what I've done then.'

I gave a sigh of relief.

It was so comforting to have someone I could trust and who knew the best way to tackle the situation. I felt a great sense of release and wandered into the ordered library. I saw I had left the book I'd brought from Race's bedroom on the chair and, with nothing else to do, settled down in the high-backed fireside chair and began to read. It was bound in leather but that had discoloured and cracked, and when I opened the book the mottled, marbled pages smelt musty.

'*The Engletons of Great Haddows*,' I read aloud from the title page, and then in smaller writing underneath, '*by Wren Paul Engleton, 1890.*'

So Wren and Paul were names that had been passed down the family, I realised.

I turned the pages and saw a great number of them had family trees, beautifully executed in italic writing. The writer had used different coloured inks, but these had faded over the years so they all blended together with only the occasional bright hue to show how the trees once had looked.

I turned to the opening pages and began to read. It seemed these were the memoirs of the said W P Engleton, written in his sixtieth year. I loved history at school and settled down to be engrossed by the Victorian historian . . .

Only I wasn't. It soon transpired that, even allowing for the era, WPE was a monumental snob and bore, who spent most of his time trying to convince the reader of the illustrious ancestors of the Engleton family!

I had once seen a TV programme which showed a tree on a medieval roll purporting to trace the family concerned back to God! But as it was the tree of a king and had been made at a time when monarchs claimed to have the divine right to rule, it was perhaps understandable.

Less so was WPE's which took some stunning liberties with the truth!

I chuckled at the outlandish claims made and flicked further on into the book. The page fell open at a passage describing Great Haddows, praising its Elizabethan origins and insisting the reason it hadn't been remodelled with the change in house styles was because of respect for the original builder, one Paul Engleton, a minor official at the court of Mary Tudor.

He must have had his eye on the main chance, because after his first wife died in childbirth, he quickly took to his side the young Anne Wren, an heiress from a lowly family, and gobbled up her money. Perhaps to please her father he called his first son Wren, and from then on, the name seemed to have stuck.

There clearly had been no documents WPE could use to describe the building of the house, so he used flowery prose and fanciful drawings of what he thought had happened throughout the centuries, becoming more believable the nearer he got to his own tenure of the house.

I had read enough about the Engletons and shut the book on my knee, from where it slipped to the floor and fell open on page fifty. As I picked it up the writing at the bottom of the page caught my eye: *The priest hole is well hidden and only those who understand the significance of the red, blue and green will ever be able to find it.*

I frowned. This meant there *was* a priest hole. I wondered where it was. There is something mysterious and exciting about finding secret places. And then

I thought, *what if Race knew where it was and had put his evidence there?* The more I considered it the more I convinced myself it was a distinct possibility.

And suddenly, I remembered the phrase Race had used when he was off his meds . . . 'Green three, blue beside, bush above; green three, blue beside, bush above!'

Had he been thinking about his hiding place? He had certainly been extremely agitated, but even then he hadn't been cognitively sound, and perhaps I was reading more into his words than they warranted.

I leaned back in the chair and considered all I knew, staring at but hardly seeing the fireplace. It was a plain piece of carved stone and as I focused on it I suddenly realised that just in the centre was the elusive date I knew I had seen but hadn't been able to remember where: 1590. I must have subconsciously noted it on the odd occasions I came into the room without really registering the fact.

Above it, running up to the ceiling, was dark oak panelling, unusual in shape and design. The oak had been fashioned into small squares, each one with either a painted symbol or a carved Tudor rose. There were green symbols in the shape of a classic lozenge, and bi-coloured ones consisting of a blue fleur-de-lys with a small yellow star in each corner. It made what could have been a very ordinary fireplace stand out.

The colour had faded over the years, so no longer displayed the brilliant hues they must once have had, but the fact that the library faced north and so rarely was filled with strong sunlight had obviously protected them, and it was still possible to distinguish which was which, even after more than five hundred years.

Just as I was musing that the panels were arranged in the diamond shaped pattern more usually seen on external Tudor brickwork, my two trains of thought suddenly collided, and I realised this could be what Race had been trying to tell me. 'Green three, blue beside, bush above; green three, blue beside, bush above!'

I counted the panels and saw there were ample to follow Race's instructions, but where was the starting point?

I counted three green lozenges from centre of the overmantel, which was also where the bottom tip of the diamond rested, moving up the right branch. Then, instead of continuing up the diagonal of the rhombus, I deviated by following the instructions and turning my attention to the fleur-de-lys beside the green panels and inside the diamond.

I realised that Race's words could just as likely have meant the panel on the right, on the other side of the third green lozenge, but as there was no way of knowing, I decided it was just going to have to be trial and error.

But what did the last two words mean? There was no panel depicting a bush. I wondered if there was some minute shrub somehow secreted above my eye level — the fireplace itself was wide and tall and I had to crane my neck to inspect the panels.

Impatient to learn more, I seized the tapestry footstool from beside the chair and moved it in front of the hearth. Stepping on it gave me a good few inches more, bringing my eyes level with the first row of panelling, but in spite of scanning each wooden tile carefully, I was disappointed not to find anything other than the two designs I had already scrutinised.

I got down again and walked to the opposite side of the room. Perhaps by taking the long view the words would make more sense. I stared and stared but the fireplace and panelling remained as inscrutable as ever. I wondered if I'd got it totally wrong — jumping to conclusions simply because of the date above the fireplace — yet something told me it was too soon to give in.

I returned to the footstool and this time ran my hand across the panels as I counted . . . 'Green three . . . ' I tapped each lozenge on the second row. 'Blue beside . . . ' I slid my hand to slide across to the neighbouring fleur-de-lys. 'Bush above . . . ' I allowed my fingers to feel the matching fleur-de-lys tile above.

Nothing! Disappointed, I decided to try on the other side. I followed the same routine and again and again the fireplace remained as it always had. But I was caught up in the possibilities by then, and tried out all manner of permutations to try and find the illusive priest-hole.

Then, as I reached out to touch an outlying panel, I slipped and slammed my hand against a Tudor rose to steady myself.

The grating noise as wood slid over stone frightened me at first. I leaped backwards and watched, amazed, as the bookcase to the right of where I was standing slid forwards over the stone floor tiles into the room as if it were a door.

I looked back at the panels. What had I done to crack the code?

Then I realised my mistake — Race

had been saying *push* not bush, and when I fell I had pushed the exact panel I had been meant to.

The open door revealed a set of rough-hewn steps winding down under the floor. I tiptoed forward. Why I was creeping about when there was no one but me in the house, I couldn't say, but the whole momentous occasion smacked of secrecy. I peered downwards.

I couldn't see very far into the depths as there was no natural light, and I certainly wasn't willing to investigate alone — I had seen too many films where the heroine was trapped in a secret compartment she had discovered when the door closed behind her when she went exploring. But what if, as I suspected, Race had hidden his evidence in this old priest-hole? Someone would have to go down to look. I knew it wouldn't be me — I was not the stuff of which explorers are made — scaredy-cats make sure they keep their distance when danger is around.

I wondered how to return the room to normal, but after tapping panels in a number of different patterns unsuccessfully, I decided it would be best if I kept the library door closed until Doug arrived — because I was quite sure he was the person best placed to take the search forward. He wouldn't be frightened of the dark and the cobwebs.

I thanked heaven I had made at least one friend in that awful house. I rushed upstairs to find my phone and once I had it, called Doug. But he must have been out of signal range and I couldn't get through. I'd just have to wait until four o'clock.

I went downstairs to get Race's lunch, first popping the baby alarm intercom in my pocket. I could hardly wait for Doug to arrive. While I waited for him I decided to find out more about priestholes, so dashed in and out of the library to get a modern book on Tudor architecture I had seen Kira reading. I didn't want to read it there — something about the gaping black hole set my skin crawling — so I carried it up to my room and opened it while sitting on my bed.

* ★ ★

I wished I hadn't as the details were pretty gruesome, but somehow, once I'd started, I couldn't put it aside.

As I knew, it could all be traced back to King Henry VIII, that despotic king who founded the Church of England in order to marry Anne Boleyn. Three of his children succeeded him: Edward the Sixth, who died at the tender age of fifteen; Mary, who tried to take the country back to the old religion; and Elizabeth, Gloriana as the poet Edmund Spenser alluded to her, and was what the troops at Tilbury were meant to have shouted in her praise after the Spanish Armada.

But Protestant Elizabeth was the Virgin Queen, and next in line to the throne was the Catholic Mary Queen of Scots. Those were dark and dangerous times, religious tension was running high, and there were many who would have supported the overthrow of Elizabeth. It was therefore made High Treason for Catholic priests to enter England, and anyone who helped them was severely punished. So priest-holes were built as hiding places for them.

Doggedly, I continued reading . . .

Priest-holes were small, with little room to stand up or move. No one knew how long the priest would have to stay there — priest-hunters or 'pursuivants' were always a danger. They would carry out detailed searches of houses they suspected of harbouring priests, counting windows both inside and out to see if they tallied, tapping on walls to find out if they were hollow, and tearing up floorboards. For the priests, the time they had to spend hidden must have been hellish — cramped, half-starved with no sanitation, it was not unknown for them to die from starvation or even from lack of oxygen.

I shuddered at the picture the book was painting. I think that part of my lack of courage can be put down to having an over-developed sense of imagination. I don't just read about unpleasant events but seem to experience them myself.

Common sense would have told me to put the book down the moment I began to squirm at the descriptions, but ever one for seeing things through to the end, I turned the pages and inspected the photos of surviving priest-holes.

By the time Doug arrived I had already thoroughly scared myself and was glad to hear his car pull up.

'I hoped you'd get here earlier,' I admitted as I met him in the hall.

'Did you?' He didn't seem very friendly. 'Did you tell anyone else about Wren's phone call?'

I shook my head. 'No, no one but you knew about it.'

He gave me a long, hard stare, which rather confused me as I was all thrilled and wanting to tell him about what I had found, and yet he seemed angry with me.

'I tried to call you, though,' I rushed on, eager to share my findings. 'I think I may have found where Race hid his evidence.'

At that his demeanour totally changed.

'What? Where?' His eyes glinted with excitement. 'Show me. Now!'

It was a definite order and I laughed at his passion. He was as keen as I was to solve the mystery and find the proof that would send the Preston family down.

'There's a priest-hole in the library.'

I took his hand and pulled him in that direction

'I discovered it by accident but was too scared to investigate any further, so I waited for you.'

'Quite right,' he said, and then, 'Phew!' as he beheld the secret staircase. 'That's certainly some find!' He walked over to it and looked downwards. 'Can't really see anything. We'll have to go down and search.'

'Well, you can, but I'm too scared,' I began, but he caught me round the shoulders, and easing me to the edge of the steps, pointed out the obvious.

'It's very small, Jennie, and I think it would be too much of a tight fit for me. I understand you were afraid to explore on your own, but I'm here now and I'll see that nothing happens to you.'

I felt sick to my stomach. I didn't want to go down into the black void.

'I know you want to protect Race, and you don't want Wren to get away with what he's done . . . '

Strangely enough, it was the sound of that name — Wren — that gave me the courage to do it. The thought that if I had gone to meet him he would undoubtedly have got rid of me so he could continue his impersonation of Paul's son, take over Great Haddows and allow the Preston family to use it as a front for their criminal activities spurred me into action. I had to do this, for Race.

'OK,' I said, 'I'll do it. But first I'm going to get a torch from the kitchen.'

When I returned Doug was lying on his stomach, head down, as he inspected the staircase.

'It looks quite safe,' he soothed me. 'Although I can't see round the bend.'

I took a deep breath. 'Let's get it over with.'

I took each step individually, first one foot on it, then the other, not feeling confident to descend any other way. The beam from the torch lit the passage, the rough bricks catching my skin now and then, causing me to wince; there were no smooth edges here.

The strong beam from the torch showed that the steps stopped where the staircase curved to the right, giving way to a narrow chamber about the height of a small man. I remembered, in the way that inconsequential thoughts invade the mind at inappropriate moments, that although Henry VIII had been over six feet tall, most Tudor men were considerably smaller than their modern-day equivalents.

I reached wooden ladder steps and, carefully, I climbed downwards. As I did so I saw an alcove set into the brick on which was a large box file.

'What's down there?' Doug shouted. 'Have you found anything?'

I waited until my feet touched the

floor and then stretched up towards the box. It was just out of reach, and as I eased it towards the edge of the shelf with my one free hand, it slipped and fell down on top of me.

My body stopped it hitting the floor but it burst open and some of the papers flew out. I tried to bend to pick them up but made the frightening discovery that the size of the chamber meant I had to remain upright; there was no room to manoeuvre. Memories of the book I had just read flooded my brain and I had to take some long, deep breaths to ease my mind. I was OK. I would soon be out and Doug was watching over me.

I shone the torch into the open box and read the front sheet of the document on the top:

To whom it may concern: Diary of Susan and Race Engleton.

I balanced the box between my body and the step so I could turn over the page, and ran my eyes over the front sheet of the diary. It didn't mince words and made it very plain how the Preston empire made their money.

'I have a diary that Race and Susan wrote,' I called back. 'And it looks like it really spills the beans on the Prestons. Wait a minute and I'll try and bring it up to you — it's a bit difficult with a torch in one hand.'

I put the torch in my mouth and gingerly climbed up the ladder, clinging on to the box file with one hand. The relief when I reached the staircase showed me just how frightening I had found the expedition, and I clambered thankfully up the stairs. Doug was waiting at the top and took the box and torch from me.

'You look dreadful,' he said as I stumbled towards the top step. 'Sit down where you are and get your breath back — I don't want you passing out.'

His concern made me feel safer. Thank heavens that was over with! I sat down where I was and handed the box up to him. He squatted onto his haunches and rummaged through it.

'This is amazing!' His delight was palpable. 'Was there anything else there?'

'Just a few papers that flew out of the box when it fell off the shelf. But I couldn't retrieve them because the chamber was too small for me to change position — it was a very tight squeeze.'

'Never mind, even if they are important, no one will ever find them, and if there is a will it must be in here.' He gave an unpleasant laugh.

'What do you mean?' I asked, confused.

'Dear little goody-two-shoes Jennie,' he said in an unpleasant voice. 'Too pure to see beyond her own face.'

'Doug, what are you talking about?'

He was making me uncomfortable and I wanted to get off the cold, hard step.

'This is what we wanted — the evidence Susan left behind that could break the family. She shouldn't have done that — goodness knows why she turned like she did — after all, she had lived a very nice life on what she later came to regard as her family's ill-gotten gains.

'Thankfully she tried to explain it all to her brother so he'd see the error of his ways. Of course he didn't, and he knew all he had to do was find the evidence and destroy it.'

A terrible fear crept over me like an icy chill flooding through my veins.

'You're talking as if you know them.'

'Know them? Of course I know them! Susan was my aunt.'

'You mean you're the head of the Preston family now?'

His face darkened.

'No, but I ought to be! My mum was old man Preston's by-blow before he and his wife had Susan and her brother. By rights, as I'm the eldest child of the eldest child, I ought to be head of the family — and its fortunes.

'Anyway, when the family needed someone to search for the evidence, I was the obvious choice as they'd already set me up in business in

Dawston so I could oversee their interests in the area — like Glandings.'

His willingness to admit to his implication worried me, because if he didn't care that I knew, I was very much afraid that meant he didn't intend to let me go. I had to try to play for time.

'The Kents will be home soon. Mary phoned me to say they would be here by five.'

That unpleasant laugh again.

'No, she didn't. Oh, Jennie, haven't you worked it out yet? Mary is my mother. My real name is Doug Kent, but the Prestons didn't want anyone to be able to trace me back to them, and as my grandfather had always supported my mother he got me to change my name.'

It was then that I suddenly remembered how I had thought he'd reminded me of someone when we'd first met. Now I knew why! And Mary had slipped up once when she'd said to me she had known Susan Engleton. If they were half-sisters, of course she would have!

So that was why Doug spent what Kira had called an inordinate amount of time at Great Haddows: he hadn't come to see the garden at all, but to confer with his parents.

'You should see your face,' he continued. 'You look like you've seen a ghost!

'You with all your highfalutin ideals about keeping Race safe — Mum was livid when Wren insisted she had to get a live-in help when the local girls high-tailed it off to university. But it would have looked odd to refuse, so she had to agree to it.

'She thought she'd chosen wisely with you, given your inexperience and lack of training, which was why she told me to take you to the dance. She wanted me to find out if you knew anything, but you didn't.'

He smirked and I remembered the phone call I had interrupted by the lych gate.

'But then you had to go and interfere. Firstly, trying to help Race get better by taking him outside and even getting the personal trainer on side — well, I had to tell Mum and she put a stop to that double quick! Wasn't I glad when you told me you thought it was Wren who had told Mum!

'And then there was all that stuff about the medication — since you'd unfortunately been to the pharmacist I told her she had to play along with you, at least to start with.'

'You persuaded her to get the doctor to do the medication review?'

'Well, I didn't have to persuade her — she knew we had to cover our tracks. You didn't think Race was normally like he is now, did you? Hmm, some nurse you are!

'Once Susan had said he had a copy of the evidence and was going to share it, we had to do something. She died soon afterwards and we wondered if she'd actually carried out her threat to make a new will. We couldn't have it coming to light when Race died — the family needed Great Haddows with all its secrets, so the search was on to find it and destroy it.

'Dr Carlton came up with the idea of drugging him — he'd always been the family physician and Race had no reason to doubt him. After all, the good doctor had supported Susan through her last illness.' He grinned. 'What Race didn't know was that Carlton has rather too much fondness for the bottle and the Prestons had got him out of a number of scrapes, so he's been on their payroll for years.'

Therefore, I realised, the over-medication had been intentional. No wonder after the review Race was simply put on different sedatives that had the same effect.

'And it was you who broke into the library, wasn't it?'

I knew without asking him, but I wanted to keep him talking — anything to stop him from doing what I was sure he intended to, that is, shut me in that secret priest-hole where no one would ever find me because no one knew of its existence.

'Of course it was.' He preened. 'I

wore black and a balaclava, so it was a shame you still caught a glimpse of me. Ma gave me a spare key and so I had no trouble getting in, but that wretched spittoon spoiled everything!'

His anger was palpable and I realised it had not been a good idea to remind him of his failure. I was coming to understand he was a man with a monstrous ego who didn't like being made a fool of.

'Then you cast dear Wren as an impostor and the night-time raider,' he continued, 'when all the time it was me, and that gave Mum the chance to move me into Great Haddows — priceless!

'We knew it would have looked odd if we'd suggested it the moment he and Kira moved out, which was why at first I tried searching when you were asleep, but you were too sharp for us.'

Again, that belligerent scowl.

So Wren *had* been trying to protect me all the time and I had spurned his help — what a fool I had been!

But I had no time to dwell on this

— I had to steer Doug away from the memory of the spittoon.

'But I wasn't as clever as you — I thought it was Wren I had seen in the orchard,' I said.

'Yes, and you thought it was Wren who had drugged your drinks.' He gave a mirthless chuckle. 'Sorry I rather overdid it the first time — you're so small compared to Race — though actually It was all to the good, since that was how you found the letter.'

There was a pause and his expression changed.

'You shouldn't have given it to Wren. It made things difficult for us, especially if he's got the ear of someone in London, as you said.'

No, I thought wretchedly, *I've made things far, far too easy for you.*

'Why did you leave the study in such a state? I would never have known anyone had been in there if you hadn't.'

Keep him talking, Jennie, *keep him taking!*

'I was fed up,' he admitted. 'Landon

276

kept calling us all to meetings in London where he'd castigate us for our lack of progress. That would set Mum off, and she'd have a go at me for not finding anything — which was rich coming from her as she's been searching for it for months! Always poking about everywhere, she was.

'But then you came along, and it wasn't as easy as it had been with the malleable local eighteen-year olds she'd employed to care for Race up 'til then.

'Frankly, I was too tired to clear up then, and as you rarely went into the library I thought I could do it later. I didn't realise I'd left the door open.'

'Did you try and come through my dressing-room door?'

I scrabbled for things to say. Anything to delay the moment when he would entomb me in the hidden chamber. But it wasn't a bright subject to bring up.

'Yes, you're always putting obstacles in my way, aren't you? You've caused us so much trouble! Mum, Brian and I have been called to so many meetings to explain what's been going wrong, and it doesn't do to get on the wrong side of my cousin! He's a chip off the old block and runs the family just like my grandfather, Trevor, used to do.'

In my desperation I decided to try resorting to feminine wiles.

'But I thought you liked me, Doug. I thought you wanted to go out with me.'

I didn't quite flutter my eyelashes at him, but I would have done if I thought it would make any real difference!

'Yeah, I knew you fancied me.'

He actually preened and I could clearly see that he enjoyed showing off about himself.

'You were OK, I suppose, but you flirted too much with that Wren. Anyway, you won't be seeing him again because I sent one of my mates down to Dawston Park to sort him out. He always said he wanted to find out what happened to his father — well, now he can ask him.'

'What do you mean?' I was aghast.

'He thought he was so smart, contacting a private dick and getting the Met interested in the place. The trouble is, if they'd started sniffing around, the crash details again they might have discovered the truth — that the engine had been tampered with.

'When Paul arrived, he was all fired up to go in to bat for his brother — he wanted Race to go into hospital for tests, which would have shown there was nothing wrong with him — so he had to be stopped.'

'But — but you're killing people!'

Doug gave his unpleasant laugh again.

'Paul learned not to mess with the Prestons, and now Wren will have learned the same lesson.'

'What have you done to him?'

I was distraught now. I had told Doug about Wren's phone call — so it was entirely my fault that he had known where to find him.

'Ah, so you're not so indifferent after all, eh? Well never mind, you'll be with him soon enough . . . in the afterlife, that is!'

With those words he stood up in one clean movement, and before I could even scream, he had slammed the door shut.

I was instantly enveloped in utter darkness.

10

It was indeed that complete darkness that got to me first. It was black, black as coal, and I couldn't even see my hand in front of my face.

I panicked and began beating against the door, but it made no difference and I realised if I was to survive, I had to manage my fear.

I forced myself to take large deep breaths, which slowed my racing heart, but even as I did so I remembered the priests who had suffocated through lack of air, which started the pounding once again.

The fear was like a nest of poisonous snakes slithering around in my guts, and a tightness round my neck as if I was being strangled. My terror of being in a confined space threatened to overwhelm me.

I sank to the ground and sat on the steps again, cold and stiff and alone. No one would come. The one person who might have done had been destroyed because of my own stupidity.

As I thought about Wren, I crumbled with sorrow. I had loved him — loved him still — and I had secured his fate. I remembered the way I'd felt when skipping arm in arm with him at the barn dance . . . the contentment I'd experienced when chatting together over coffee . . . most of all, the sheer excitement and anticipation of desire when I'd realised I loved him.

I rocked back and forwards in my misery as I accepted I'd never be enfolded in his love again.

Time dragged on.

The trouble with being somewhere without indication of day or night is that you have no idea how many minutes or hours have passed.

I always wore a watch but it wasn't a digital one, nor even luminous, so I had no inkling of what time it was, though my body gave clues that it was quite a while.

It was extremely cold despite being mid-summer, and for a moment I played the glad game and thought how fortunate I was that it wasn't winter. My gratefulness did not last long — my back ached from where I was leaning forwards and hugging my knees in an attempt to keep warm. My head ached, and I smarted where my skin had been grazed by the rough brick walls.

I knew I had to stay positive and tried to think of happier times. I knew from when nursing my parents that joy can come from the saddest of moments, but it was hard to find anything to celebrate when locked underground in a dark stone prison.

I asked myself if I regretted coming to Great Haddows, and although I would have given anything to be somewhere else at that moment, I thought of meeting Wren and caring for Race, and realised there had been a great happiness as well as the sadness and fear.

Race! It hit me like a ten-ton truck

— now the Prestons had Susan's evidence, there was no need to keep him alive.

I knew now that what I had mistaken for Mary's fear when Race had his chill had not been concern for his welfare, but worry that he might die before they found the evidence that could unmask them. I couldn't bear the thought that there would be yet more killing — and all because I had trusted the wrong man!

I forced myself to stand up, and sharp pains shot through my legs as the blood ran back into them. I thought about the book I had been reading and wondered at the bravery of those men who had risked severe discomfort and death for their beliefs. They had gone willingly into their hidey-holes; I had done all I could to avoid mine.

I leaned back against the coarse bricks, being careful not to move my feet lest I was on the edge of a step and slipped. It was hard not to cry.

After a while I stretched gingerly and

manoeuvred myself round until I could rest my side against my jagged support, flinching suddenly as my hip pressed against it. I had forgotten my altercation with the linen-bin the night before and now I had developed a throbbing bruise. I straightened immediately and shot my hands out in front of me to press against the bricks on the opposite side to stop myself from falling.

Once I had got my balance again and my heart had stopped beating out a tattoo, I went to rub the offending bruise. My hand touched something hard and square in my pocket. The baby monitor! What a shame it wasn't a two-way radio. I stuck my hand in to my pocket and withdrew it . . .

That's when I saw that it wasn't the baby monitor, it was my phone! I must have inadvertently stuffed the wrong device in my pocket, as they were about the same size.

I'm not ashamed to say I started to cry — but tears of relief. There was hope after all!

Only when I felt steadier did I open the case and press on the home button. Light flooded the hole and immediately I felt a little better.

I held the mobile up to my face and was dismayed to see the words *no signal*. Desperately I moved my arm around the brick prison, all with the same result. No matter where I moved it, the outside world remained tantalisingly out of reach.

The only place I hadn't tried was the actual chamber itself, and I didn't want to go down there again. I argued myself out of doing so until I could find no reasons not to — after all, if death is the only alternative almost no fear is too great!

I sat on the bottom step before climbing onto the ladder and descending.

I tried the phone again and after several attempts, suddenly found that if I held it in one corner, just two small bars appeared on it. Not the greatest, but probably the only chance I'd get.

Without thinking I hit Wren's number, and it was only when his voice kicked in on the answerphone that I realised no one would be picking up his phone — and why.

I was about to hang up when I reasoned that if the phone had accepted the call, it still had to be working, and as Wren had been in partnership with an ex-policeman, there was a small chance his phone would be found and examined.

I decided to leave a message just in case it was . . . I gave my name and explained, as briefly as possible, what had happened and where I was. Most importantly, I described how to open the priest-hole — though I'm not sure I would have understood the instructions had I been listening to myself, such was my hysteria.

I rang off and then decided to call the emergency number, nine-nine-nine. I lifted my arm to check I still had a signal and that's when it happened . . .

My fingers were sore from holding

onto the mobile so tightly and, as I tapped in my security code, my aching fingers gave way and I dropped the phone!

I heard it clatter to the ground so loudly in the complete silence, and then my own voice screaming, 'Oh, no!'

I couldn't believe what had happened. My one chance of rescue was gone!

Even if the phone was still working I knew I wouldn't be able to pick it up — I had tried with Race's papers and had discovered the chamber was just too narrow to allow me to bend my knees, hips or back, effectively meaning the mobile was now out of reach. I looked down and knew that very soon the battery would run down and I would have no way of contacting the outside world.

It was too much! I had done my best to stay positive and cheer up myself along, but the futility of it all overwhelmed me. I pulled myself up the ladder to the staircase, and there I collapsed on the steps and sobbed until sheer exhaustion overtook me and I fell into an uneasy sleep.

I dreamed that I was being chased by an enormous digger, its bucket snapping at my heels as I ran, with Doug laughing manically in the driver's seat. Ahead I could see a man on a motorbike weaving from left to right as he tried to avoid being caught, and I was all that stood between him and oblivion. My lungs were burning from the chase, and my muscles ached from running. I was slowing down — I couldn't keep going — soon I would be overtaken and Doug would do his worst.

'No! No!' I shouted aloud as I woke.

At the same moment the door above me swung open and blessed light flooded in.

'Easy, darling, easy.'

The voice was achingly familiar, but I knew I must be hallucinating. Then two strong arms were slipped around my waist and I was dragged out of that hell hole.

'Wren?' I didn't understand. 'I thought you were dead.'

'And that's exactly how I thought I'd find you.'

Expertly he slipped his arms under my legs and lifted me out of the priest-hole, then carried me to a chair.

'I couldn't have forgiven myself if anything had happened to you.'

I gazed at him with astonishment. Should I take his words to imply that I meant something to him, or was it simply that he regretted not having been able to persuade me to leave?

'Doug told me he'd sent someone to kill you.'

'He did, but luckily the Met had become very interested in what was happening at Great Haddows and decided to stake out the park for our meeting. When Doug's henchmen turned up and started threatening me, they were there in a flash and arrested him.

'Once he realised the police were looking at a case of double murder — that of both of my parents — he decided he didn't want to take the rap for Doug and started singing like a canary, as they say.'

'And the police now recognise the crash wasn't an accident? Doug admitted as much to me.'

'Yes — when they re-opened the case and went through everything with a fine tooth comb it became obvious. Linking Doug to it will move things forward, though we're no nearer finding proof of the Preston family being actively involved.'

I made fists of my hands and banged them on my head. 'If only I hadn't been so stupid as to trust him! I found the proof and handed it straight to him!'

'You weren't stupid, he was very plausible. I wish you had trusted me a bit more, though.'

I blushed. How could I have doubted him?

'So how did you know where I was?' I asked. 'Did my answerphone message get through?'

He smiled. 'It did — and well done

for explaining the riddle of the fireplace so well. It took us a while, but we eventually worked it out.'

I looked around and saw that the 'we' included a number of uniformed police officers.

Fear gripped me. 'Race?' I asked.

'Is fine and upstairs. When we arrived, Doug wasn't here and as there was no one to look after him, the police called an ambulance. He's going to be taken to hospital for tests.'

'Wren, Mary is a Preston. Susan was her sister and Mary was born illegitimately to old man Preston before he married, but he always supported her. And Doug is her son.'

'Phew. That's some story! You'd better tell the detective chief superintendent here exactly what Doug told you,' he said, indicating with his open palm a grey-haired man in a suit standing to one side of him. 'And then the minute you have, you should go to bed.'

'I couldn't stay here, not on my own!' I was sure of that.

He gave me an inscrutable look. 'You won't be alone, I'll be back. Do you trust me now?'

'Yes, I do,' I said, and I knew I always would.

* * *

I spent an hour with the chief superintendent, recalling all I could of my conversation with Doug.

I was lucky that he had been so keen to tell me how clever he had been — I realised he'd wanted to boast about his exploits and as I wouldn't be able to tell anyone, he had said a great deal.

At last I had exhausted my memory and made my way upstairs to bed — but not before I was reassured that Mary and Brian had been arrested on their return on suspicion of drugging Race.

'Sleep well,' Wren said as I made my way upstairs — and I did, knowing he was there.

* * *

The next morning when I first awoke I wondered why I felt so relaxed and happy, and then I remembered . . . Wren was sleeping along the hall.

I gave a leisurely stretch and winced as my sore muscles complained of their poor treatment the previous day.

I climbed out of bed and looked out over the Kentish garden and its waves of colour and lush growth, a haze of mauves and blues and greens.

I walked to the dressing-room where the linen-bin was firmly in its position as guardian of my virtue. I had placed it right against the door before I went to sleep, but whether to guard myself against Wren or to guard him against me was a moot point!

The relief I had felt when I realised he was not dead had been so intense that I knew without a doubt that I would never love anyone else as I did him, and I hoped he might feel something for me . . . I was sure he had called me 'darling' when he found me in the priest-hole.

But his behaviour since then, while comforting and kind, had given no hint of passion. Perhaps he only saw me as a friend.

I took care getting dressed that morning. Normally I pulled on jeans and a top, scraped my hair back into a ponytail and left the rest to nature, but knowing Wren would be seeing me at the breakfast table encouraged me to make a bit more of an effort.

I put on a pair of cotton trousers and a brightly coloured T-shirt, allowing my hair to bounce loose around my shoulders. I even added a touch of make-up and a quick spray of perfume — very subtle as I didn't want him to think I was making an effort especially for him, even though I was.

He was casually dressed, sitting at the pine table, steaming coffee cup in hand. I thought he looked magnificent!

'How are you feeling?' he asked and I said I was much better. 'The detective chief inspector rang me earlier. They caught up with Doug on his way to

London in his very fast car.'

'I thought it was rather a grand vehicle for a small businessman when he took me to the barn dance,' I remembered.

'You can bet it came from ill-gotten gains! He was stopped on the M25 and they relieved him of the box file. The police are going through it now but are disappointed that whereas the diary accuses the Prestons of many nefarious activities, it gives no proof, and nor does anything else in the file. Your testimony will help, of course — but as it stands, there's no real evidence.'

At that moment the sun went behind a cloud and it seemed to me it was in sympathy with how I was feeling.

'So they'll get away with it — the crash, everything?'

'Not everything. It has been established now that the crash was not an accident, although it's uncertain who arranged it. And Mary will be prosecuted for drugging Race, but without hard facts, there's little more they can do.'

I poured myself some coffee and

stood with it by the back door. I remembered all the high hopes I'd had about improving Race's situation, and actually I hadn't managed to do it at all. Once his medication was under control it was doubtful he would need me any longer, and I wondered where I could go.

'I suppose you and Kira will be returning to South Africa?' I asked.

I tried not to dwell on how I would feel when he was thousands of miles away. Why did it matter how far he was, anyway? He gave no indication of having any feelings for me, so really it was all the same if he lived next door or in Cape Town.

'Maybe,' he said. 'We want to sort Race out first. I know he has a life interest in Great Haddows, but I don't think that living here is likely to be conducive to his health. Since the Prestons own it, I think he'd be better moving back to South Africa with us.'

So there it was — I'd have to get used to a future without him.

'I must phone my friend, Jean,' I said. She would know what I should do. 'Oh!' I remembered. 'I dropped my mobile in the priest-hole and couldn't pick it up because it was too small to bend.'

'We can go and get it now.' Wren stood up. 'I'll help you.'

'You'll be too big.'

'Well, I could hold you by the legs and you can go down face first to retrieve it.'

There was no way I was ever setting foot in that place again, and I said so.

'You don't have to — you'll be using your hands!' he smiled, but then seeing my fear, became serious again. 'Look, I've got a walker's headlamp that you can put on to light your way. I keep one in my pocket now I have the motorbike; you never know when you're going to have to carry out repairs by the side of the road in the dark.'

He laughed again and I knew he was trying to relax me, but I didn't find it funny.

'I can't!'

'Don't you trust me, Jennie?'

Of course I did. I nodded.

'Then let me help you. You're too precious to me. Don't you know I'd never to allow anything bad to happen to you?'

I stood stock still and stared at him. Had I just heard correctly? Did he call me precious?

He held his hand out to me and I took it.

All at once I was enfolded in his strong, safe arms. He bent his head and I saw that his green eyes held an expression I had never seen there before: love.

Then his lips met mine and I knew then that I had found the love of my life.

'We'll get your phone together,' he said, and we went to the library. He tapped the code into the oak panels and the secret door slid open.

My heart was pounding as I started down the stairs. I did trust Wren, but I was still afraid, and had insisted we propped the door open with one of the fireside chairs before we entered.

When we reached the ladder, I placed my hands on the top rung. Once Wren was holding my legs securely, I descended hand over hand. The headlamp lit the cobwebs of hundreds of years and nestling in a corner was my very dead mobile phone. I reached down and grabbed it, pushing it in my pocket.

Scattered around the floor were the papers that had flown out of the box file. It looked as if they might all have been part of a single document at one time. I picked them up, dust of ages and all, and stuffed them under my T-shirt.

'OK,' I called, 'pull me up.'

Slowly, one hand after another, I rose up the ladder until I was safely on the steps.

The open door allowed some light in, but I still wanted to get out as fast as I could. I brushed myself down well away from the fireplace and divested myself of the now somewhat crumped sheaf of papers.

Wren started to smooth them out.

'Good grief, Jennie, do you know what these are?' His eyes were shining with excitement.

'No. I didn't get a chance to look at them.'

'*Last Will and Testament of Susan Engleton*,' he read. 'This is amazing! I'm no expert but this document certainly gives credence to the idea that Susan wanted to make amends. She's left everything to Race — 'to carry out the plans we have discussed which are appended to this document with the reasons why I wish this'.'

It all began to make sense, now.

This was what the Prestons had feared Susan had written, and what they wanted to get their hands on. Presumably previous wills had left everything to them, in line with the fact that their money had saved Great Haddows and paid for the many companies run from the house. But by leaving everything to her husband, Susan had cut them out of the equation and ensured Race would be able to carry out her wishes.

'No wonder the family had been searching if they thought she might have made a new will,' I said. 'They couldn't risk it turning up at a later date and exposing their criminal activity.'

Wren pointed to the pages.

'And the reasons she talks about gives all the evidence the police need. She's put it all here, in black and white. I must phone them to come and collect it . . . ' He slipped his arm around my shoulders. 'But let's go out into the garden first.'

He took me out to an old wooden bench under a pergola. Roses rambled above us and birds sang and all was well with the world.

'What will you do, now you know the Prestons don't own Great Haddows?' I asked him as I settled back in his arms, the gauzy delight of nature soothing me as gardens always did.

'If Race wants to stay here — and I hope he will — then I might, too. There's a lot to do to clear the Engleton name, and I'd like to help him do that.'

'And Kira?'

'I think she'll stay, too. She got quite engrossed in all the family history stuff she's been investigating and I'm sure she'd would like to find out more about the Engletons. I think she needs roots.'

'Everyone needs roots,' I agreed.

He took my hands in his.

'I want your roots to grow with mine,' he said. 'Do you think they could do that, Jennie?'

'That depends on whether you and Kira still believe I'm so stupid you could pull the wool over my eyes,' I teased. 'Are you sure you want to make roots with such a gormless person?'

'What? Oh, we didn't mean it like that! What we were afraid of was that Mary had chosen a carer without experience because it would be easier for her to pull the wool over your eyes to maintain the status quo.

'She ruled the local girls with a rod of iron and brooked no interference, and we were sure her lack of care for Race was part of the problem. But we had to tread very carefully as we were only staying here on sufferance.

'We were looking for proof of what had really happened to Race and to our parents, but we had to watch our step. It was only after she accused us of being the cause of his agitation that we saw how dangerous she was — and initially we thought you had joined her, too.'

'You weren't very complimentary . . .'

He had the grace to flush. 'I shouldn't have doubted you,' he said, 'and later I was so concerned when I couldn't convince you to be wary of her.'

'Well, I can't complain since I doubted you too.' I thought for a moment. 'Did you always suspect Doug? I heard Kira say she thought it was interesting that he was took me to the dance.'

Wren appeared embarrassed and looked down at his feet.

'We did wonder about him, but no, we weren't suspicious of him at first.'

'Did Kira fancy him, then? I just wondered why you both gate-crashed our set at the barn dance.'

'No, she didn't fancy him as you so colourfully put it, but it *was* about fancying *someone* . . . you see, I was the one doing the fancying . . . Jennie, I was attracted to you the moment I first saw you — and Kira knew it.

'I so wanted to take you in my arms at the dance, but then when you appeared to be getting friendly with Doug, I tried to keep out of temptation's way. But Kira is protective of her big brother and was annoyed when you seemed to prefer Doug, so she decided to engineer things so that we swapped partners.'

He had a sheepish expression on his face.

'That's why I was interested when it appeared you were falling for him — and why I gave you a wide berth after that.'

I was flabbergasted. So that was why he had been avoiding me! 'I never would have guessed!'

'Oh, Jennie, you are such a straightforward person! And brave and caring.'

'But I'm not,' I insisted, 'not brave, I mean. I've been absolutely terrified most of the time!'

I didn't want Wren to be disappointed when he realised what a coward I was.

'Not brave? You?' He let out a great guffaw of laughter. 'Don't you know that is what bravery is — being afraid, but going ahead anyway? I don't know anyone braver than you.'

It was such a surprising thought — that scaredy-cat Jennie might actually be brave! I thought about what he said and realised I liked this new description of me.

'Absolutely,' he said, and pulled me back into his arms. 'And just so there's no misunderstanding, I love you very, very much and I want you to spend the rest of your life with me. Is that plain enough?'

'Yes, quite plain enough, thank you,' I said, grinning. 'And that's exactly what I'd like, too!'